SIDEWINDER FLATS

When horse trader Con Carnigan's cavalry horses are stolen, he faces starvation if he cannot retrieve them. He tracks them to Sidewinder Flats in the Sonoran Desert, but finds himself in the domain of a western Fagin. The town is a robbers' roost run by Hoffman, who offers Carnigan the sheriff's job, so long as he turns a blind eye to the criminals. Carnigan however, takes the job seriously, as Hoffman and his cohorts discover . . .

Books by Walt Masterson
in the Linford Western Library:

TOMBSTONE LULLABY

WALT MASTERSON

SIDEWINDER FLATS

Complete and Unabridged

LINFORD
Leicester

First published in Great Britain in 2007 by
Robert Hale Limited
London

First Linford Edition
published 2009
by arrangement with
Robert Hale Limited
London

British Library CIP Data

Masterson, Walt
    Sidewinder flats.—Large print ed.—
    Linford western library
    1. Western stories
    2. Large type books
    I. Title
    823.9′14 [F]

    ISBN 978–1–84782–510–0

Published by
F. A. Thorpe (Publishing)
Anstey, Leicestershire

Set by Words & Graphics Ltd.
Anstey, Leicestershire
Printed and bound in Great Britain by
T. J. International Ltd., Padstow, Cornwall

This book is printed on acid-free paper

For my wife, Helen, who went with me up the trail to Fort Bowie

1

When Carnigan saw the smoke rising from the cabin, he knew he was in trouble.

The cabin was miles away and several hundred feet lower down the mountains, and unless one of his horses had learned how to light a fire the smoke meant there was someone in his place.

He could not see into the valley he called his claim, but he knew exactly where the cabin was, tucked back against the wall of the mountain near the waterfall which irrigated the valley, and that smoke was right where he ate his breakfast.

Carnigan was not expecting visitors, but then Apaches or Pimas were an ever present possibility, and every time he left the valley, it was possible that he might get raided. He accepted the risk like he accepted the possibility of snow or drought, and lived with it.

Today, though, was different. The hunting had been good this fall and the warriors had been busy stocking their stores for the winter. Most of the troublesome Apaches had been pushed south by Crook's activities to the north, and the valley was well away from the normal trails.

Of course, it was always possible that a wandering young buck eager to blood his lance could happen by, and disappointed by the lack of a victim, loot the place and set the fire out of pure spite. The Apaches, after all, had plenty to be spiteful about.

But there was not all that much smoke, and any self-respecting raider warrior would be ashamed to do so little damage.

He ground hitched his horse and tied the pony, whose wandering ways had dragged him away from his ranch, to a tree. He could not rely on it to stay ground hitched like his saddle horse, and he had spent quite enough time catching it and bringing it back anyway.

He built himself a capful of fire from a bundle of dried cactus skeletons, and made coffee, and chewed jerky while he waited for the coffee to cool enough to drink. It would be a couple of hours before he got back to the valley and, in that time, the raiders — if raiders were responsible — might even be waiting around for him to come back. Best eat while he could, and be ready to run if he had to.

At least he had two fast horses with him, he reflected. The obvious target for raiders would be his herd of horses. He captured and trained them for the military and had a contract to deliver them saddle broken at the fort within the month. He needed the money badly, and the loss of the herd would be a heavy blow.

The smoke did not thicken and spread, but went on rising in a thinning column and by the time he had emptied the coffee grounds over the embers of his fire and kicked dirt over the burned spot, it was just a haze.

He mounted up and, taking the buckskin in tow, rode on down the mountain towards his ranch.

★　★　★

The horses were gone, all right. Both the saddle stock he had been breaking for the army and his own little herd of mounts. He leaned on the saddle horn and surveyed the ranch from the fringe of the trees near the waterfall.

From here, the buildings looked undamaged. His house was unburned, though smoke still eddied from the chimney and the barn, which doubled for a stable seemed untouched. The poles of the corrals were down, one of them smashed, and the corrals both empty.

When he was reasonably sure, he rode up, approaching from along the foot of the cliff, and stepped out of the saddle when he was close enough to see that the front door of the cabin was open, and the shutters left swinging. He had closed both when he left the previous day to hunt down the buckskin and bring it back to the ranch.

His caution was unnecessary though. The house had been broken into and his stores ransacked, and his spare guns and store of ammunition taken. Somebody had cooked themselves a meal and eaten it at his table, before kicking over the bench and throwing the blankets from his bed onto the fire. His clean clothes were gone.

When he took to the hills after the missing horse, he had taken his camp gear, so he had blankets to sleep in, a skillet to cook and a water bottle and a skin for the horses. His spare harness had been taken and his spare boots, which made him swear mightily. He had worked long and hard for those boots, and had had to ride to Tucson to get them.

In the barn, his spare saddle, curiously, was untouched, and so was the rack of equipment for caring for his horses. He walked round examining them and, so far as he could see, nothing was damaged.

So the purpose of the raid had been to steal his horses, and that meant that somebody knew they were there, and that they also knew he was away from the ranch.

He stopped and looked thoughtfully at the buckskin. He was a restive horse, inclined to roam when he was not watched, but even so he had wandered a remarkably long way on that particular occasion. Had he been deliberately set free and chased off? If so it was a very effective way of getting Carnigan away from his ranch, and it had worked.

He saw to the horses and tied them up inside the stable once they had been rubbed down and watered. Then he saw to himself.

The raiders had taken all the stores in sight in the main cabin, but they had not discovered his safe cupboard behind the chimney breast, so he refilled his ammunition belt and put some boxes of cartridges into his saddle-bags. His leather coat he had been wearing on the mountain, so he had adequate protection against the weather if the thieves had gone high.

He thought about it over his bacon and beans. He had seen no tracks around the valley lately, though with so many horses in his corrals a new set of tracks would have been almost impossible to find.

Whoever had raided him knew he had stock right enough, and knew what state of training they were in. So, he had been scouted by somebody, and that somebody was not an Indian, because an Indian would have burned the buildings.

No, he had been raided by white men, and white men who knew the right time to hit him. The horse gather was finished for the summer season, and the stock had been saddle broke and trained, roughly at least, to the saddle and bridle.

He swore again under his breath, and poured himself more coffee. The night was already falling, and there was no point in trying to track before first light. He would get a good night's sleep and start in the morning. It would give the raiders twenty-four hours start, but that would have to be borne.

He spent the rest of the evening repairing the damage left in his home, and hiding his spare gear again in the space behind the fireplace, and rolled in his blankets in the barn with the horses. He was going to be keeping them company for the next few days anyway, and the three of them might as well get used to it.

★   ★   ★

Dawn found him already at the notch which served as a gateway to the valley, and in which the tracks of the stolen herd could clearly be seen. They had been taken by at least three riders, for he found three sets of horse tracks

8

which were identifiably different from the shoes he fitted to his own horses. There could be more, of course, but three men could work the herd easily enough. Thanks to weeks of work, they were more easily handled than raw wild stock.

He wondered at first if the rustlers might take the horses to the fort and sell them as their own caught and broken stock. But the longer he followed them the more clear it became they were not going anywhere near the military.

Instead, they were driving south and west into the Sonora Desert. Down there conditions were savage and hard on stock, and the only reliable water he knew of which would be of use to the thieves was at Sidewinder Flats. He tucked his head into his collar against the growing hot wind, pulled his hat down over his eyes, and turned the horses' heads towards the town whose reputation was as poisonous as its name.

It was going to be a long haul and the stolen horses would need to be rested and watered on the way. They could not be simply pushed onwards continuously. The thieves had gone to such trouble to plan and execute their raid they would have planned for the journey as well.

On the way down to the Flats there were several tanks at which the stock could be watered, though such a large herd would severely deplete the water and, until rain came again, the trail they were taking would be made dangerous for unsuspecting travellers following in their footsteps and relying on the tanks.

At the thought, he dismounted, and gave his animals a drink from the water skin. It was healthily full at the moment, but he knew it would not see them to Sidewinder Flats. He would be relying on at least some water having been left in the tanks and he had the uneasy feeling that the rustlers would see to it that there would be as little as possible.

He was right. When he got to the first of the tanks, a deep cleft in rocks, overshadowed by a low cliff, he could see the hoofprints of many horses and the water had been drained down to the bottom of the natural storage basin. There were a couple of puddles in the deeper part of the cleft, and he let himself down to test it, relying on his saddle horse to hold his weight against the rim.

The water seemed sweet enough, though it was clouded by sand, and he was about to fill his canteen when his eye caught the shape of a rattlesnake through the murk.

He flinched back with a sharp intake of breath, then saw that the snake was not moving. A prod or two with his knife told him the creature was dead and beginning to rot, which in turn told him the water was contaminated.

Carnigan climbed out of the cleft and swung into his saddle. The poisoning of the water might of course be accidental, a result of a natural occurrence, but whether it was contrived or not, it made the waterhole useless for weeks.

The next one was several hours along the trail and, when he reached it, that one, too, had been drained. This one was a shallow basin in the shade of a grove of desert trees, and by digging down into the wet sandy bottom, he managed to raise enough water to fill his canteen. This time there was no dead rattler in the water, and it smelled and tasted sweet. He took an experimental swig, and waited for an hour with no ill effects before letting the horses drink from the refilled hole. The water seeped in reluctantly, and he had to take the mounts to the hole one by one.

There was still a long way to go, however, and he would need another water source before he finally got to Sidewinder Flats. Reluctantly, he turned his horses' heads towards the line of low lying hills to the south. Up there, he knew, there was another tank, miles out of his way, difficult to find and even more difficult to use, but reliable water known to few. Pima Indians knew of it, of course, and probably Apaches, too. But he had no choice.

As he turned his horses south, he had the distinct feeling he was being watched. It was strong enough to make the skin between his shoulder blades itch, and he trusted that itch. It had saved his life more than once.

He shucked the rifle out of its boot behind the saddle, and levered a shell into the chamber.

2

The Chiricahua was a youth, just achieving manhood, and he needed to prove himself. He had been seeking a lion to kill with his lance, or even a bear, but a white man was far better and had the asset of being equipped with all the treasures an Apache youth could dream of.

A white man — this particular white man at any rate — had a repeater rifle, at least one shoots-six, two good horses, a fine Bowie knife on his belt, and there were bags loaded on the back of his led horse. The Chiricahua boy prepared his attack with great care.

First, he needed to catch the white man unawares. This was not usually too difficult, since a white man generally lacked the desert-born almost mystical sense of identity with his surroundings. White men could be watched for long periods without sensing their enemy's attentions.

The boy tracked the white man on a parallel course, not following his tracks but always able to observe his quarry. A couple of times the man with two horses dropped behind a ridge or a rocky outcrop and was for a moment out of sight, but he always reappeared just where he should be and he showed no hint that he was aware that he was being followed.

The Apache recognized where the white man was going before they were even halfway there. He was aiming for the tank on the side of the low mountain ahead, which also meant that he knew something of the desert. Few white men even suspected its existence and the ones who did usually stayed well away. It was impossible to get water out of the tank without exposing the drinker to attack.

But the youth was impetuous and eager for his first kill. He knew that the safest time to make his bid was when the white man had to turn his back and bend down to reach the water.

If the quarry knew he was being stalked he would not turn his back, and that would make the kill twice as difficult. But this man showed no sign of the slightest suspicion. He merely rode on an entirely predictable and exposed route.

It meant that the Apache could see him at almost every stage of the journey, though the open nature of the land meant he also had to keep a safe distance away. He did not worry about it. The time to take his scalp would come when the man had to enter the hilly territory which surrounded the tank.

The day wore on and it was mid afternoon when quarry and hunter in turn entered the narrow canyon which led to the outcrop under which the water was to be found.

Just before it reached the tall rock which overhung the tank, the canyon took a sharp kink to the left followed by an equally sharp bend to the right, and the Apache was forced to lose sight of his prey.

He was not worried. There was no side canyon into which the man might disappear. If he went in at one end, he must perforce come out at the other. For the first time the Indian closed the distance between them and when his target disappeared from his sight round the first bend, he hurried his mount to catch up.

He had his bow in his left hand and two arrows clasped tight against it. A third was held between his teeth and, as he rounded the sharp kink in the canyon, he dropped his gaze to nock this third arrow to the bowstring.

The thrown Bowie, twelve inches of razor-sharp heavy steel, backed with a thick bone hilt, entered his chest just below the point where his ribs separated and struck immediately into his heart. With his last dying gaze, he lived just long enough to see the man he had been planning to kill and rob sitting his horse just round the bend and pulling his pistol from its holster.

★ ★ ★

Carnigan grabbed at the Indian pony's halter as it started to turn away in surprise, but he missed and the Apache fell backwards over its rump. He hit the ground as dead meat, and Carnigan dropped from his horse with the Colt clutched in his fist but not needed.

He swore as he crouched over the corpse. Killing a teenage boy gave him no pleasure, and only the fact the young warrior had been planning to kill him made it tolerable.

He pulled the corpse out straight, and recovered his knife. The combined speed of the throw and the Indian's own forward movement had driven it to the hilt in the chest, and it took all his strength to disengage it from the wound.

Carnigan pushed the body into a gully worn by one of the desert downpours, and kicked the edges of the trench in over it. If the boy's people found him they would do the necessary rituals over him. By their lights he had died an honourable death, stalking an enemy.

The tank was as he remembered it, tucked low under a great slab of rock which almost cut it off from the outside world. To get at the water, he had to lie down on his face and slide under the rock, then drop the canteen into the dark depths and use it to fill the water bag, and then finally itself. His skin crawled while he was under the rock at the thought of the snakes which might be under there as well, but no rattle rustled in the gloom and, when he probed with his rifle, no scaly head appeared to investigate.

He watered the horses, drank slowly but deeply himself, and was surprised at how cold it had remained. The heat was going out of the day now that the sun was down, and before long the cold would be bitter. He needed a campsite and he needed it well away from the water before the desert creatures came to take their evening drink.

He already knew the spot he wanted, but he was also aware that it must be known to the Indians and probably other desert-wise travellers. However, both were scarce, and by the law of averages it was unlikely that they would be around now.

When he arrived at it, the little basin in the rocks was empty sure enough. He pulled on his coat before he started his tiny fire with a bundle of kindling he had picked up on the march. Against a slab of stone as a reflector, it threw its tiny heat back at him and boiled his coffee efficiently enough. He drank and ate camp-fire bread and bacon before scouting the surroundings for one last time and wrapping himself in his blankets. The horses, tethered on short ropes, ate their bait of oats and hay, and stood, hipshot, nose to tail.

Guarded by their superior hearing and natural nervousness, he slept.

* * *

Sidewinder Flats sat in the middle of the desert and simmered. Though the year was coming down from its summer high temperatures, the Flats seemed somehow to embrace the heat and cuddle it to its heart.

In the early afternoon, wise men and careful women took to their beds in curtained rooms and perspired, because to open a window was to fry. The animals in the corrals on the outskirts of town drank from their troughs and drank again.

Just who had originally tapped the spring which made Sidewinder Flats' existence possible, no living men knew. There were stone basins around the spring which had been old when the Spanish had ranged the land, sweating in their steel backs-and-breasts and high-combed helmets.

Now, they had been turned to the task of keeping the little town and its inhabitants and their stock alive. Not comfortable, not enjoying life, but alive.

Carnigan and his horses arrived across the burning desert desperate for some of that water and, at the public trough in the centre of the street, the horses were allowed to drink sparingly while Carnigan filled his canteen at the ever-running rill which fed the old stone basin.

Sidewinder Flats owed its existence to the springs and every now and again it would occur to some passing candidate for power that the man who controlled the water supply controlled the town, and one or two of them had tried to take over the precious springs. The slow-moving ones, and those who thought they could cow Western men and women with the threat of violence, were buried in what the town called its Boot Hill outside the huddle of shacks and buildings on the downwind side. There was no hill, a local wit once remarked, but there sure as shootin' were plenty of boots down there.

The town's single street was flanked

on both sides by a straggle of homes, a trio of false-fronted saloons, a general store and a surprisingly lavish barber shop and public bath house. At one end of the main street and back from the buildings was a huddle of shacks and lean-to huts.

There was a restaurant called Polly's, a gunsmith and harness store, and what the town called a bank, but which was in fact just an adobe cube which contained a steel cupboard with a padlock on it. The cube was also the home of a man who called himself Ambrose Smith, who spent most of his time sitting on the stoop of the Hoffman House, the town's most central saloon and by far the most lavish one.

In the Hoffman House, a traveller would find Hoffman. He was a fat, florid man who wore a fancy silk waistcoat over a white shirt and black trousers. His boots were as highly polished as a New York banker's, his sleeves confined by a pair of dancehall girls' garters, and his hair was carefully combed forward to disguise the fact that it had been receding for some years.

It did not conceal it, but nobody ever laughed at Hoffman's little vanity. Laughing at Hoffman was one of those rare, non-habit-forming vices, because people who laughed at Hoffman finished up in Boot Hill, still wearing their boots.

Yet there was on the face of it nothing frightening about Garside Hoffman himself. He smiled constantly and laughed easily. Every man who came to his table tucked into the alcove under the staircase of the Hoffman House was guaranteed a drink and offered a cigar.

He presided over a perpetual poker game in which the players changed constantly, though there were always cards on the table and piles of chips which waxed and waned as the cards fell.

Every now and again, he would ask, genially, for a moment's privacy, and the card players would put down their hands and move to the bar while he talked business with one man or another who happened by.

At the end of the talk, the stranger would play a hand of cards. Sometimes, he would win and take a pile of chips to cash in at the bar. More often, he would lose and pay up with surprisingly good grace.

The progressive poker game never seemed to end, and Hoffman never seemed bored by it, while the talk at his table was always amusing at least to the players, for laughter and good fellowship seemed to surround them.

An observant man — or, more often, woman — would notice after a while that while Hoffman always seemed the first to laugh in his deep, rich voice, and to be the first to call for more drinks or a new pack of cards, his broad, fat smile never reached his eyes. They remained always cold and watchful as a rattler on a rock and as devoid of human warmth or pity.

'He reminds me of a spider,' one saloon girl confided to her friend. 'He sits and he watches and he waits and the flies come to him and he eats.'

Her friend knew what she meant and she knew how to endear herself to Hoffman, for she related the conversation to him later and the ill-advised saloon girl found herself having her head held under the water at her weekly bath. They buried her in Boot Hill the following morning, one of the few people ever to drown in the middle of the desert, which did at least give her some distinction in the town.

Carnigan found Hoffman a fascinating study. He left his horses at the town's smithy and livery stable, a flourishing business with a constantly changing set of customers riding suspiciously good horses, and took his saddle-bags to the Hoffman House.

Hoffman noticed him arrive and pass through the archway into the lobby of the hotel side of his business and noted the smile of the bar tender, who doubled as hotel receptionist, which meant that the new customer had paid for his room in advance.

He noticed, too, that when the newcomer came down the stairs, having left his bags in his room, he had washed and combed his hair. And he noticed the long barrelled Colt .44 tied down on Carnigan's right hip.

And he wondered.

★   ★   ★

'Passin' through?' asked the bartender, as he poured Carnigan's first drink. It was a schooner of beer and had a whiskey chaser next to it, though Carnigan had not ordered the whiskey.

He looked at it and then raised his eyes to look at the barkeep. The man grinned.

'Courtesy of Mr Hoffman,' he said, nodding at Hoffman as he did so. Carnigan turned to look at the saloon owner, received a genial wave of the hand, and raised the shot glass to toast Hoffman.

'Mr Hoffman says will you join him,' the barkeep relayed, swabbing the bar busily. 'He likes to talk to folk passin' through. Says it keeps him in touch.'

Carnigan nodded. 'Makes sense,' he said, in a neutral tone of voice, glancing over again at the table under the stairs. Hoffman's smile was as wide as all outdoors, and his gesture of invitation would not have been out of place in the court of a caliph.

Picking up his schooner of beer and the whiskey, Carnigan took him up on his invitation. Hoffman's fellow card players got up as he approached, and nodded at him as they passed on their way to the bar.

'Sit down,' the fat man invited. 'Rest your legs. Come far?'

He studied Carnigan as he talked and found nothing remarkable about him. Carnigan was a tall, long-boned man with wide shoulders which stretched the material of his shirt, a shock of dark hair which needed cutting and a couple of days' stubble on his chin.

He wore jeans, a dark checked shirt and a soft leather vest which fastened at the front with a thong. His Colt revolver was worn at hip height supported by a plain leather cartridge belt the loops of which were all full. He had a pair of soft leather gloves folded and half stuffed into one hip pocket. His bandanna was silk and had seen a good deal of service. So had his hat, a low-crowned, flat-brimmed felt hat which had seen plenty of weather.

His boots were old and worn and he had Mexican spurs with large rowels and a length of loose chain which chinked slightly as he walked.

A typical cowpoke, by anybody's standards.

And yet . . .

And yet there was that about him which made him different. An air of more than usual watchfulness, maybe. A level, direct look about the grey eyes which made a man think twice about him.

Hoffman was a good judge of human

beings, and had relied on the accuracy of his judgement for many years, yet he could not quite place this one.

The man he was studying returned the scrutiny without a change of expression.

Hoffman saw an enigma. Carnigan, like the late dancehall girl, saw a spider. A large, well-fed spider sitting in the back of his web and enticing passing flies into his trap.

So he waited, and after a little small talk which was mainly Hoffman asking disguised questions, and Carnigan telling him the least he judged necessary for the man to know, Hoffman considered he had a mental sketch of the newcomer.

'Goin' to be in town long?' he asked. Carnigan studied the whiskey glass, which Hoffman noticed was hardly depleted at all.

'Depends,' Carnigan said.

'Anything I can help with?' asked Hoffman idly.

That got him a reaction. Carnigan

looked directly at him and Hoffman found the stare disconcerting.

'How?' said Carnigan.

'Can't say until you tell me more. What do you need?' said the saloon keeper. 'Work? Lodging? Advice? Money? I loan money on the right security.'

Carnigan shook his head. 'Never borrow,' he said flatly. 'Could do with work, though. What you got?'

The fat man shrugged and spread his hands. 'Name it!' he said. 'The Flats is a growing town. We need a good carpenter. Got no plumber. Most of the men can knock a building together, but nobody knows how to metal a road. We always need more stockmen. I employ a number of security men to guard my holdings, and anybody who is better than the normal with a gun can get a chance with me. You got any experience with the law?'

Carnigan grinned tightly. 'Which side of it?'

'The enforcement side! We get troublemakers through here, time to time, and we came up short a sheriff a week or so back. Gang of drunken bad actors ran him out of town on a mule and he never came back.'

'What's the deal?'

'For the right man — fifty a month and found. You have to be good with that' — he gestured with his cigar at the Colt. 'You get to bunk down in the back of the office, and there's a couple of cells back of that. Office is across the street a block down. Interested?'

Carnigan laughed. 'Might be a new experience, bein' on the other side of the star! Don't you need references? If not, when do I start?'

The fat man assessed him under lowered brows, and found himself still at a loss. He decided to take a chance; after all, there were plenty of men around town who could rectify a mistake for him overnight.

'Forget the references. Jed!' he called.

A voice shouted, 'Yo!' from the other side of the bar, and heads turned to watch as the barman brought over a tin box. Hoffman opened it and emptied the contents on the table.

There was a bundle of papers, a writing pad and a bundle of keys and finally a silver star with the words SHERIFF and SIDEWINDER FLATS stamped on it. Hoffman picked it up and threw it across the table.

'Needs a meeting of the town council, technically, but I can take responsibility until the next one. Isn't for a month or so, but I reckon if you prove yourself, there'll be no argy-bargy,' he said. There was a strange sparkle in his eye as he said it, and Carnigan could hear, in the curious hush which had fallen on the bar, a stifled snort of amusement.

Hoffman's expression flickered minutely, but he straightened his face immediately into its habitual amiable smile.

And Carnigan had become sheriff of Sidewinder Flats.

3

The new sheriff of Sidewinder Flats sat in his office and cleaned his rifle. The exercise was not necessary. The Winchester was perfectly clean, lightly oiled and had not been fired since the last time he had cleaned it. A perfectionist might well argue that since then he had ridden through a dusty desert and it was as well to be certain it would not jam, but he would be looking for an excuse.

The real reason was that when he had to do some serious thinking, Carnigan cleaned his gun and, at this moment, he needed to do some very serious thinking indeed.

Apart from the theft of his horses, none of the events of the past few days made any real sense to him, and the thought made him very uneasy.

The theft itself was understandable

enough; they were good horses, and already saddle broken. But could the rustlers have known that? It was the manner of the raid which disturbed him.

First, the theft of his horse herd was obviously very carefully planned indeed. His ranch was not exactly hidden up in the Dragoons, but it was well off the beaten track, and there was only the one obvious entrance to the valley, which was in itself hard to find. Even Carnigan had come across it by accident.

In short, the men who had rustled his horses must have known they were there, and come specifically to steal them. They had come in exactly the right strength to steal the herd: three men who knew how to handle horses. Two to drive the herd and one to scout.

They would be experts, too. Horses were far more independent than cattle and harder to keep under control and moving in the required direction. Yet the thieves had lifted them and pushed them along without difficulty.

So they knew he was there, knew about his horses, and knew he would not be around when they lifted the herd. That meant that the wandering pinto pony had not just meandered off of its own accord, but been freed and driven.

That had pulled him away from the place for just long enough to steal his herd. Since the trail had led him right here, and he had arrived with the very paint horse the thieves had used as a decoy, the thieves knew he was here.

If they knew, so did Hoffman. Carnigan guessed that nothing happened in the little town that the fat proprietor of the Hoffman House did not know about. Knowledge seemed to be his business.

He finished polishing the firing mechanism of the rifle, then started on the barrel with a pull-through and some oil. The calico in the pull-through came out clean, of course, but he ignored the fact and went on cleaning until he had done it six times. It was a ritual.

He had not missed the sudden snigger from the boys at the bar when he accepted the sheriff's star, and he had a shrewd idea he knew why they found the fact funny. The one thing about a sheriff was that he was usually to be found in the sheriff's office, and when he was not in the office he would be out on his rounds. In a place as small as Sidewinder Flats, that meant within a square half-mile.

The badge was not just pinned to his shirt. It also pinned him down.

If the previous sheriff had been run out of town — and Hoffman had not said he left, merely that nobody had seen him since — the only place he could go was the desert. Next town of any size — pretty well the only town at all — was Yuma where the prison was located. Yuma was a long, long way away across the desert.

He finished cleaning the carbine, and reloaded it with its full thirteen shells and let down the hammer gently. The rifle version of the Winchester would have given him a little more range and four more bullets in the magazine, but the extra four inches in length made it more awkward to handle on horseback, and Carnigan spent most of his waking life on a horse.

One of the things which resulted from being made sheriff was that people would know where he was at any time of the day or night. It would also make him a target for any troublemaker who happened by, or any assassin who might be hired.

On the other hand, it also gave him a reason for wandering where he wished around town, and asking any question he liked of whomsoever he chose. It also lent legality if he found himself facing one of the men who had stolen his herd.

He went through the wanted notices on the board in the office. At least two he recognized from the bar in the Hoffman House, so he had at least a start on knowing the trouble makers by sight.

And he was already certain there would be trouble, probably within the next twenty-four hours.

He laid the carbine on the table and took his spare pistol from its place in his bed roll. It had not been exposed to the dust of the trail, so he contented himself with wiping it over with the oily rag, and loading the sixth chamber which he usually kept empty and under the hammer. The risk of an accidental discharge was at the moment far less than that of running out of shots at a vital moment.

Outside, it was going dark in the unnaturally sudden way of the desert, and he put on his gunbelt, tied down the tip of his holster and pushed his spare pistol behind his belt buckle.

Then he lit the lamp at the back of the office, let himself out onto the street and began to make his rounds.

It did not take long. Sidewinder Flats was small, and the only area which made him wary was the huddle of shacks and sheds at the west end of the street. They had been pushed together with whatever wood was available, which was not much, and weather-proofed with tarred paper and canvas. Half of them were little more than tents with one side pushed up against the nearest solid wooden wall, and if one of them caught fire, which was a likely event, there was nothing to stop the fire from running from one end of the area to the other.

He walked warily around the huddle of shacks, which was already buzzing with chatter and the occasional shout. A woman wailed somewhere in the middle of them and was answered with brutal shouting.

Carnigan stopped in the shadow of one of the more solid buildings in the mass, and waited.

Before long another shadow fell across the narrow alleyway between the shacks, and the whisper of clothing brushing on the wooden side of one of them told him he was being stalked.

Carefully, he hunkered down where

he was and drew his spare pistol from his belt. In a situation like this, with short ranges and cramped conditions, he would have preferred a shotgun, but the rack in the sheriff's office was empty, and he had not brought one himself.

For a second, a shadow flickered across one of the lighted windows in the alleyway, and he heard the faint jingle of a spur chain. Then there was silence, and he knew the man following him was also keeping still and listening.

Further up the alley a door opened, and light spilled out. It was behind the stalker, and Carnigan could see him clearly in silhouette, then the door closed again and darkness returned.

Carnigan stayed where he was, listening in the gloom, and once again heard the whisper of cloth brushing against wood. Then a light at the end of the alley blinked as somebody passed across it, and he was alone.

Whether the man had seen him in the light from the opened door, or whether having been exposed, he had thought the better of his stalk, Carnigan simply did not know, but he was gone.

He swore to himself, left it for another couple of minutes, then heard an altercation starting at the other end of the huddle of shacks, and headed towards it cautiously.

However, whatever had been going on was over by the time he rounded the corner, and only a couple of Mexicans were to be seen on the main street, making their way on horseback towards the far end of the town where the corrals and the livery stable were located.

He stood in the dark against the store front, and listened. Behind him were the muffled sounds of the shanty settlement, and from the saloons came the plinkety plonk of pianos. From the far end of the street came the sound of somebody playing a guitar, some sad Spanish tune from the sound of it.

For a town full of bad actors, it seemed remarkably quiet and sounded almost too normal.

Suddenly, he decided not to sleep in the sheriff's office tonight. Instead, he collected his bedroll and walked down into the desert outside the grove of straggly trees which surrounded the springs. He had noticed a patch of broken stones and shingle out there and, in the middle of it, he laid out his blankets and rolled himself in. Rattlesnakes avoided broken pebbles like these, and anything bigger could not cross them without making a noise.

Listening to the sounds of the desert night, he closed his eyes and was instantly asleep.

★   ★   ★

There was a frost on his blankets when he awakened in the first light of dawn, and he lay there for a minute listening to the sounds of the desert around him. There were rustlings, and the curious ticking sound of the desert stones beginning to shed their frost. He shook out the blankets carefully to make sure there was no scorpion or spider in them, and rolled them tightly and tied the thongs into place around them.

Sitting on the roll, he shook out his boots vigorously and was rewarded with a startled scorpion which flew out of the left one, hit the ground running and vanished among the stones. The discovery made him doubly careful with the right boot, but it was empty and he pulled it on.

Standing up, he stamped around to get the boots settled, slung on his gunbelt and rolled the cylinder in the Colt to hear the pawls click solidly into place. The spare revolver he tucked behind his belt buckle again, then walked back into town by a roundabout route. If anybody had been watching him in the night, chances were they knew where he had slept, but if they did not, he did not want to draw attention to it.

There was smoke coming from the chimney of the little restaurant, so he pushed open the door and walked into a warm, cheerful room with red and white gingham tablecloths and the smell of frying bacon and coffee.

There were half-a-dozen men eating, sitting at a long table which occupied the centre of the room. Down the side, there were a few tables for four people, two of them already occupied by men and their womenfolk.

A pretty woman in a gingham dress which matched the tablecloths smiled at him from the counter at the end and pointed to one of the unoccupied tables, and he followed her direction and sat down, leaning his bedroll and rifle against the wall behind him.

She had seated him at the table near the counter, and he was able to sit with his back to the wall, shielded from behind by the high counter, and facing the door and the room. He wondered if the position was a deliberate choice by her, or a happy coincidence.

The woman came around the counter

with a cup and saucer and a big tin coffee pot in her hands.

'Howdy,' he said, with a grin, and she smiled back. The smile lit up her face and he felt cheered by it.

'What can I get you, Sheriff?' she said. 'We got bacon, beef, beans, frijoles, and this week I got eggs as well. Name your pleasure, and no wise-cracks, unless you want your next coffee down your jeans!'

There was a guffaw from the men sitting at the communal table, and Carnigan gathered from their covert grins that one customer at least had come in for the coffee treatment. From the steam which rose from the big pot, he guessed it had to be meted out only once.

'What you just said sounds great to me, ma'am!' he said. 'I like the eggs over easy, and I'll take the coffee in the cup, if you please.'

She winked at him, poured the coffee and retired behind the counter, where he heard pans being rattled and the

46

sound of bacon and steak sizzling.

The coffee was good and so was the chance to sit, apparently staring out of the window, but in fact evaluating the room

The men at the centre table were the mix he expected to find in any town in the south-west: a party of miners, some stockmen and a couple of wagon drivers, the men who made the town work. The blacksmith was at one end of the table, sleeves rolled back over massive forearms, and the marks of burns from flying sparks over his exposed skin. He was sipping surprisingly daintily from a cup.

Next to him was the bartender from the Hoffman House. He looked up at Carnigan and nodded recognition, though he did not stop eating. Few men in the territory talked over meals. The consumption of food was considered too serious a business to be interrupted.

But the ranchers and their wives were a different matter. One of the men in Sunday-go-to-meeting clothes eating with their wives caught Carnigan's eye and nodded.

'Morning, Sheriff!' he said. 'Gonna be here long?'

There was a ripple of what Carnigan was beginning to recognize as Sidewinder Flats 'private joke' amusement, and he caught a few sly glances under lowered eyebrows.

'Depends,' he said drily. 'Some lawmen rest and move on. Some stay permanent.'

'Very permanent!' murmured one of the drovers, a slender man with lank hair and a drooping moustache, and there was a rustle of amusement. The wit stuck his hands in his bright red suspenders and sniggered.

Carnigan grinned along with it, and marked the man for future attention. He had an air of secret knowledge, and a sly cast to his eye.

'Some put down roots,' he agreed.

'And some get planted,' said the sly-eyed one. There was another guffaw of laughter, and once again Carnigan joined in. He really must have a chat with this one, and that right soon.

His breakfast arrived and he devoted himself to demolishing it. It was very good, and there was a lot of it, and he was just polishing his plate with the remains of a hunk of bread when the last of the other customers paid their tab and left.

The woman in the red gingham brought over the coffee pot to refill his cup and he pointed at a chair.

'Join me, ma'am?' he invited. 'You sure are the best cook I come across in a long, long while!'

She smiled and brought herself a cup as well, and sat down with him.

'I'm Jenny Rennes,' she said with a challenging cock to her head. 'So let's get the wisecracks over right away, please. It's a long time since I heard a new one, and it wasn't very funny even then.'

'Not told by the wiseacre in the red suspenders?' he said with a grin, and she nodded.

'Right first crack out of the box!' she said. 'How did you guess?'

'Somehow, he had it written all over him,' he said.

'Many more cracks, and I'll carve it across his chest with a blunt skinning knife,' she said. 'I'm here to pay off a debt, not to give him a target for his wit.'

'A debt?'

She put her forearms on the table either side of her coffee cup and hung her head suddenly. Then she snapped upright, again.

'A debt to Hoffman,' she said. 'Didn't you know? All of us are paying off something or other. Aren't you?'

He stared at her. 'What d'you mean, all of you?'

She waved her arm towards the street in a sweeping gesture.

'Nearly all, I should have said. We — Joe and I — were on our way west to the coast. California, we wanted. He was a carpenter, and a good one, too. I was a teacher. We were working all the hours God sent back in Georgia, but the carpet-baggers had taken the lot, and nobody had money to pay. We scraped enough to buy a wagon and a team, and we joined a wagon train and set off.'

He waited till she had refilled his coffee cup, watching her face. There was no sign of self pity in it, just a matter-of-fact expression.

'We got this far. Well, not quite this far, but nearly. A sidewinder got one of the oxen. There really are sidewinders here, you know. We cut him out of the traces, and the remaining three got us just past the town boundary, there. Then the axle broke.'

Her composure wavered for a second, and he waited while she got herself back under control.

'Joe went into town to find a carpenter who would supply wood for a new one, and while he was gone, I heard shooting. Not much, just a couple of shots. I didn't think anything of it until the men came.'

She lowered her head and swallowed hard.

'They told me Joe got into a gunfight in the saloon and had been killed. He hadn't been gone more than a half-hour, and he hadn't got his gun with him. It was under the seat in the wagon. I didn't like him carrying it, and he left it there because of me.'

Carnigan could guess the rest of the story, but he listened anyway. Bewildered and terrified, she went to the sheriff's office, and a man with whiskey on his breath told her that her husband had been playing cards and had lost a good deal of money.

'They said he pulled a gun — he didn't have his gun with him, so how could that be? — and was beaten to the draw. I had to pay for his funeral, and the man he had been playing cards with claimed what money I had, plus the team and the wagon, against the debt.'

Carnigan nodded. 'There were witnesses, of course?'

'Four of them. Mart Dooley and the

one they call Pima Frank Smith. They are members of Gutierrez' gang. He's one of the bad men who run this town, and Tex Buchan is the other. They both work for Hoffman.'

'And Hoffman was a witness to the card game.'

'Oh,' she said, her eyes clouding. 'You heard already.'

He shook his head.

'In a way I heard, yeah. I heard this tale in rough towns all over the world, ma'am. New boy in town gets shot, and his wife is told he was playing poker. Or blackjack, or any one of a dozen games, makes no difference.

'What never varies is that he lost, and the widow, or the parents, or his sister, are told they have to pay up. And they start paying, and they go on paying until there ain't nothin' left. No money, no home, no stock if he was in cattle.'

She stared at him. 'You know about these things?'

He shrugged. 'I'm the sheriff. Of course I know. Was the last sheriff involved in this?'

'No, his predecessor. This town is hell on sheriffs. They never last longer than a few weeks, and then there's a new one, usually the next stranger into town. How did you guess?'

He was watching the street with narrowed eyes.

'I been sheriff of towns like this 'un, ma'am, several times. The names and the saloons change but not much else. And now' — he hitched his gunbelt round to his hip — 'we're about to get a visit, and I wish you'd to stay out of it, ma'am. It's me they're after. Stay out, no matter what they say!'

As he spoke, he stood up and moved out from behind the table. There was the sound of boots on the boardwalk and the door was pushed open.

4

The first man through the door made a real sidewinder look cuddly. He was a man of medium height but so broad across the shoulders that he appeared short. He had tight ginger curls which emerged down the back of his neck in thick coils, and had been so heavily soaked in scented oil they looked almost liquid.

His eyes were pale blue, and his eyebrows and lashes so light they were almost invisible. He was wearing ordinary range clothing, but on his feet he had heavy cleated boots like a lumberjack.

Behind him came two men who might as well have worn labels saying BAD MEN in red capital letters. The one thing they all had in common was an eager, mocking look about the eyes.

This, thought Carnigan, is the first

hassle. He dug his makings out of his shirt pocket, pulled out a cigarette paper and made it into a deep gutter, into which he started to tap tobacco. To outward appearances, he was totally absorbed in the task, and the three men began to spread out across the room.

To spread his targets might have looked like a good tactic, but in this room with its long central tables and chairs, it put two of them the other side of heavy boards from him, and the walls of the restaurant constricted their ability to move round it.

Carnigan rolled his cigarette, licked the paper and twisted the end, then put one end in his mouth. His eyes met the pale, deep-set ones of the ginger-haired man.

'Ain't no smokin' in here,' said Ginger.

Carnigan reached back with his left hand and pulled a match from his pocket, then struck it against the seat of his jeans.

'I said — '

'Sure, you did. I heard you. You said: 'Ain't no smokin' in here'. Heard you myself, clear as clear. So what?'

The ginger man grinned more widely. He began to move to a clear space closer to Carnigan, and Carnigan suddenly realized why the man wore heavy, cleated boots. He was a kicker. With those shoulders and the short powerful legs, he would be a formidable adversary, and the cleats would make him a terrible one.

'Which one are you?' he said. 'Buchan? No, I bet you're Gutierrez.'

He saw the man's eyes widen, and knew he had hit a raw nerve. He guessed at Buchan, and that the man would take being mistaken for a Mexican as a gross insult. The massacre at the Alamo was still raw in the minds of Texans.

'Kind o' light skinned for a Mex, ain't you?' he said drawing heavily on the cigarette. 'First one I ever seen with red hair, too, but it's sure greasy enough.'

57

He saw the man begin to move, and held out one hand with his palm outwards.

'Before we get started,' he said, 'let's get one thing straight! I kill you first. No matter who pulls the gun, I kill you first! Then you and then you.'

As he said each 'you' he pointed directly between the eyes of each of the gunmen, without taking his gaze from the ginger-headed man. Each man saw the gesture and the accuracy of the pointing finger. Each could see quite clearly the message behind that finger. If it had been a gun, he could be dead.

'O' course, one of you might get a shot off,' said Carnigan.

For the first time Ginger's sneer faded slightly.

'One of us would be bound to get you,' he said. 'You're dead!'

'Maybe,' agreed Carnigan. 'But you won't care, and neither will he. You will both be dead.'

He deliberately pointed at the two behind the table in a different order.

They both started to correct him, glancing at one another, before they realized how ridiculous it was.

'We'll get you, easy,' said Ginger. He was still shuffling his feet to try and get into position for what Carnigan was certain would be a crippling kick.

'Bet your life?' he said, and grinned. Out of the corner of his eye he saw one of the flankers start to move sideways stealthily, and said sharply, 'Keep still, or you'll kill him. He goes first, no matter who draws.'

Ginger's eye flickered, and unconsciously, he started to reach out a warning hand towards his two cohorts.

'Keep still,' he snarled. 'We can do this later.'

'Later would be good,' Carnigan told him, good-naturedly. 'Later would be favourite for you. You can stay alive, till later at any rate. Choose life — or choose Boot Hill.'

By now he had worked his way round to the door and, as he finished, he stepped smartly through it, and immediately walked down the side of the structure to the rear. He heard running feet cross the floor and the door open even as he stepped out of sight of the main street.

But they had lost sight of him, and in the tangle of alleyways of the shanty town, he lost them, too.

No shooting, which was good, and no bullets in his hide, which was better. But he had only postponed the inevitable. They were too used to having their own way, and had got sloppy. None of them had really assessed the layout of the room. In an open space they could have rushed him and at the very best he could have got one before they had him.

Now, he was in open space and they knew where he would be at least at some time in the day, because he would have to go back to the jail.

But he was still perplexed. Why make him sheriff if the intention was to kill him? Why not just shoot him and have done with it? He was certain that at the very least somebody had recognized his horse in the livery, and knew who he was.

Knew, therefore, that he was not a casual drifter who had taken the star to earn travelling money. Knew instead that he was a robbed rancher after his stolen stock.

He walked down to the stable and saddled the pinto. It was a horse which needed exercise, and it was just about to get plenty, so it came with him willingly, though he was certain that out of the corners of its eyes it was just looking for a chance to make for the horizon.

It was not that the horse was untrained — he had trained it himself and it knew how to behave — it just got the devil in its soul and took off for the far blue yonder when it saw its chance.

He rode the horse over to the corrals where the stock was being held. There was some shelter from the heat because of a sprinkling of cottonwoods nearby, and his own horses were bunched in the shade of them, nose to tail, flicking at the flies with their tails and occasionally stamping their hoofs with the irritation.

One of them, a pretty little sorrel mustang he had picked out for the commanding officer's daughter at the fort, recognized a reliable source of sugar lumps, and made her way over to him, to nuzzle his shirt pocket through the bars. He palmed her a lump of sugar, and pulled her ears gently while she nodded her head.

Through his feet he could feel approaching hoof-beats, and he reached down and slipped the loop off the hammer of his pistol. He waited until the hoofs were close behind him and swung instantly into the saddle facing the approaching two men on horses.

They were strangers, and they looked at him through hostile eyes, men in range clothes and battered hats, one of them carrying a rifle in his hands.

They pulled up when he faced them, hands resting on his hips and only inches from the butt of his gun.

'Yeah?' he said.

'What you doin' here?' said the man with the rifle.

'I'm checkin' over this here stock. They yours?'

Both men looked slightly discon-certed. Now that he had turned, they could see the star on his belt, and for some reason they had not known he was the new law officer. They were disconcerted, but not really bothered.

'Didn't see the star, Sheriff,' said one. 'Have to be careful round here with the stock.'

'You sure do,' he agreed. 'So these ain't yours then?'

The two men exchanged glances. The situation was clearly not to their liking, but they had hurried over when they saw him examining the stock, and there had to be some obvious reason for it.

'They're not ours yet,' said the taller one, carefully. 'We was thinkin' of buyin' them today. Just rode out here to look 'em over. What do you think of 'em?'

He affected to look the animals over,

but did not take his eyes off the two men.

'Fine horses,' he said. 'They'd be a good buy for any man with the money. Cost a lot, though. How much you offerin'?'

Again the exchanged looks, then the spokesman said, 'Ain't made an offer, yet. What do you think?'

Carnigan shook his head dubiously. 'Myself, I'd stay clear of these horses, boys. Look like stolen stock, to me. Who's sellin'?'

That caused a flutter of embarrassment, as he had suspected. Neither of them wanted to name a horse dealer who might also be a rustler. Life around Sidewinder Flats, as he was discovering, balanced on the edge of a very sharp knife.

'If we name them we're callin' them horse-thieves,' said the talkative one. 'Thing like that can get a man killed around here. You find out for yourself, Sheriff. We're out of this one.'

The two wheeled their horses, and

set off at a canter towards town, looking back over their shoulders once they felt they were out of range. The encounter had not gone according to plan, and it showed.

But Carnigan felt no further forward. He had found his horses, but if he tried to take them away, he would be pursued as a horse-thief and could very easily be hanged for stealing his own stock.

He needed to find the rustlers and they were somewhere in town. They might well know what he looked like, in fact must know since they had scouted his claim and been there long enough to take this very horse away and draw him off for the theft. So he had to assume they knew who he was.

He ran his hands over a couple more of his stock, but the rest were absorbed into the herd in the corral and he had neither time nor inclination to separate them out.

Also, it was unlikely that the would-be horse buyers would leave the matter lying. They would be bound to go back to their seller and, at the very least, warn him that the sheriff was interested in the horses in the corral. They might even have handed over money already for them, in which case they would want it back.

He turned the pony's head towards the open desert, and made a cast across the burning plain. The little town was surrounded at a distance by mountains, and there were mountains to the southwest which reached high into the hot air.

The Sierra del Cabeza Prieta it was called, and he treated it with respect. Beyond there, he knew was the brutally hard Malpais.

Fort Yuma and the new prison they were calling Hellhole were down that way, but the badlands were as good as sentries, and there were always the Indians.

He headed north of the town, and dropped into a dry wash. It kept his progress from watching eyes, and he had to assume that he could be watched at any time.

The wash swung round the town on the east side, and probably kept it from being flooded in the summer monsoons. It was deep and wide enough to carry a lot of flood water, dumped from the mountains and, what was not carried past the town probably went into the aquifers which produced the miraculous springs which gave the town life.

It was while he was examining the walls of the wash that the first bullet thumped into the ground in front of him. The report came a split second later, and was followed by another.

He did not wait to find out where the third one went, for he was lying along the neck of the pinto, spurring it hard, and the horse, outraged, was racing, belly-down, along the sandy floor. He distinctly saw one and then another fountain of sand whip upwards out of the floor, then he was round the corner of the dry waterway, and reining in the horse.

He pulled the carbine from the saddle boot, and turned the horse back to the bend in the wash, examining the far wall carefully. There was more than one gunmen, he knew, but he was not sure whether they were both on the far side of the wash, or if at least one was on this side.

He found out almost immediately that there was one opposite, for the man stood up, staring in the direction he had gone. The man's calfskin vest was a piebald black and white, and would be easy to recognize again and, when he moved his head, his hat gave off a strange glitter as though the brim were on fire. After a moment, Carnigan realized it was made by a metal hat band. Carnigan tucked the horse back against the side of the wash, let his hat fall back on his shoulders, held by its chin string, and stood up on the saddle to see over the bank.

The second shooter was standing up, searching the wash with rifle poised in his hands, ready to shoot, and his gaze had passed over Carnigan's head even as it came into his field of vision. He gave no indication he had seen it.

They were certainly not from the same bunch that had braced him in the restaurant. But they were equally certainly looking for him, not just any rider.

He wondered whether the woman in the eating-house had put them onto him, but doubted it. She seemed to be trapped by circumstances, and not a part of the town's setup.

Far more likely, he thought, that the two men he had met by the corrals had passed the word that the new sheriff was showing an unhealthy interest in the horses they wanted to buy, and whoever was selling them had decided to eliminate him on principle.

There was also the possibility — probability — that one of the original thieves had seen and recognized him, and decided to get rid of him straight away.

The rifle across the wash fired and

fired again, though where the bullets went he had no idea. Certainly they were nowhere near him, and he resisted the temptation to shoot back. For one thing, it would have meant betraying his position, and for another, he was not certain how many shooters were out there.

Whatever, he was going to have to do something to clear up the situation, or no matter how careful he was, someone, sometime, was going to get lucky and Sidewinder Flats was going to have a vacancy for a new law officer.

He moved the horse along the side of the wash, and climbed up on the saddle again. This time he found himself right behind a cholla plant, its thorns sparkling like frost in the desert sunlight.

He treated all chollas with respect. This one, however, hid his head, which was a lucky break because he was right in the line of sight of the rifleman this side of the draw.

The man was crouching, rifle halfway

to his shoulder, while he watched the edge of the dry waterway. There were another couple of shots from the other side, and Carnigan realized the rifle opposite was trying to flush him out for the man this side to get a clear shot.

Up to this point, he had been concentrating on staying away from gunplay until he could work out who represented who in the town, but he could feel himself getting mad. He had been robbed, threatened, lied to and shot at, and he was fed up with the whole business.

He put one foot on the saddle horn, his hands on the edge of the steep bank, and vaulted up onto the flat ground. There was a startled yelp from the waiting marksman, who had obviously been expecting him elsewhere, and he started to swing his rifle into position.

Carnigan shot at him, and then threw himself flat, rolling sideways three times. There were two shots from the opposite side of the wash, but they did not come near him and, when he looked, he could no longer see the marksman from this side.

What he could see though, was the man's rifle, lying across the rock he had been using as a shooting rest, and while he watched, it wobbled and slowly slid off the rock at this side.

Carefully avoiding the cholla, he scrambled round until a rock was between him and the other side of the wash, and risked a quick survey of the near rifleman's position. He found that from his new position he could see a hat lying on the ground, and the rifle lying in front of the rock. But there was no sound.

'Dooley?'

The call came from the other bank. It was not answered from this side.

'Mart? You there?'

Still nothing. Carnigan carefully surveyed the opposite side of the wash, and after a few moments was rewarded with a flicker of movement, but before he could get his rifle to his shoulder, there was a sound of hoofs on the desert floor, and dust told him the shooter had gone.

Had he run off, or was he merely changing his position? Carnigan had no way of telling, but he took no chances. Staying as flat as he could, and keeping a wary eye open for scorpions and snakes, he crawled to a point where he could see behind the marksman's rock.

From his new position, he could see a pair of boot soles, toes to the sky, lying still behind the rock and, keeping his head low, he approached and saw that his snapped shot had been lucky enough to hit his ambusher in the chest.

The man's eyes flickered open when Carnigan leaned over him, and the man licked his lips. There was a lot of blood in the dust under his body, and since little had come out of the hole in his chest, Carnigan guessed the bullet's exit hole was a big one.

The eyes focused on him then the man gasped, 'You got some water, mister?'

Carnigan examined him carefully for a hidden weapon, but he could see the man's handgun lying on the rock, the rifle had fallen the other way, and in any case, he seemed strangely still. His hands lay lax by his side, and though he moved his eyes, he did not roll his head at all.

'You got water?' he asked again.

Carnigan's canteen was on his saddle, and his saddle was on his horse, which he hoped had not pulled its regular running off trick. He walked back cautiously to the rim of the dry watercourse, and found the horse still standing where he had left it.

He dropped to the saddle, rode it round to a less steep part of the wash, and up onto the desert. The sniper was lying where he had left him, and the guns were in the same position, so he got down, and took the canteen to the man, and held it to his mouth.

The man drank a little, but the effort brought on a coughing fit he plainly had trouble with. There was blood running from the corner of his mouth, and when he coughed it brought a bright froth to his lips.

His eyes met Carnigan's.

'Lung shot?' he asked in a strained voice. Carnigan nodded.

'Good one for a snap shot,' the wounded man gasped. He had still not moved his hands or legs, so the wound was obviously not just a lung. It must have hit his spine, as well. Maybe he had been turning when the slug hit him.

'Where'd you come from?' asked the dying man. 'Ain't seen you around before, I'd bet on it! Why'd they want you dead? I thought you was just a pilgrim passin' through that fell for the sheriff's badge trick like the others.'

'Trick?'

'Sure. Hoffman always tries to have a sheriff on the books, keep the gangs from hittin' on him. The lawmen don't last long, but while they're here, takes the heat off Hoffman.'

'I thought it was Hoffman's town,'

75

said Carnigan, though he was beginning to have a glimmer of understanding.

'It is,' gasped the dying man. 'But there's a few folks don't see why it has to stay that way.'

'Who?'

The eyes were clouding, and he could hear the blood bubbling in the man's throat.

'You're Dooley,' Carnigan said, into the dying man's ear. 'Who was the other guy?'

There was a flicker of spite in the gunman's face. He strained to raise his head from the ground, but without success.

'He'll get you,' he gasped. 'He's hell on wheels with a gun. He's called . . . '

But the effort of issuing the threat had been too much for him. The eyes went blank, and the jaw fell slack.

5

The afternoon was well on when he rode into town with Dooley's horse trailing behind him. He hitched it to the rail by the sheriff's office, got down, and walked across the street to the general store.

Inside the place was a surprise. By contrast with the dusty, run down exterior, this was a smart, well stocked store. There were racks of shirts, jeans, boots, and a whole wall of bolts of cloth. There were racks of tools, a case of knives, a glass counter with a selection of handguns in it. The usual piles of cans, bottles and sacks took up the body of the store, and there was even a jar of candy sticks on the counter.

A tall, bald man in his shirt sleeves and a floor length apron was checking a list in a ledger, and looked up when the door opened. His face was wary, and when he noticed the star pinned to Carnigan's belt, it got warier.

'Yeah, Sheriff, what can I get you?' he said, tonelessly.

'What happens to cadavers in this town?' said Carrigan.

'Depends,' said the storekeeper. 'Mostly, they finish up in Boot Hill.'

'Who puts them there?'

The man tucked his pencil back behind his ear, and put down the ledger.

'Undertaker,' he said.

'Who's the undertaker?'

'I am.'

Carnigan looked him over carefully, and nodded.

'What say we kind of start over?' he said. 'Let's leave out the smart alec single word answers and cut to the chase? That way, I won't get mad and you won't get to wish you'd bin a mite smarter. I got a dead man name of Dooley belly down over his horse outside. Plant him!'

The storekeeper shrugged and pointed at the back of the store.

'Bring him round back. I'll look after him there,' he said, and called loudly to the back of the store. 'Martha!'

There was a female squawk from somewhere in the depths of the building.

'New sheriff's started his business already! Got some for you, too!'

A door opened and closed at the back of the store, and a stout woman in a tight black dress appeared, looping a tape measure round her neck. She looked surprised when she saw Carnigan.

'Oh! Hello, Sheriff,' she said. 'Know his name, this cadaver you're bringing in?'

'I gather it's a man name of Dooley,' he supplied and both of them looked surprised this time.

'Mart Dooley? One of Gutierrez' men?'

'Don't know his first name. We wasn't that close,' he said drily. 'But if

Mr Gutierrez had a thin man with a snaggle tooth workin' for him, name of Dooley, he's got himself a vacancy right now.'

The storekeeper shook his head dolefully, though his expression was surprisingly bright.

'Gutierrez ain't goin' to like this a-tall!' he opined, and his wife nodded bright agreement like a robin on a spade.

'He will be put out considerable,' she said. 'He says that touching one of his men is like touching him. He'll take it real personal.'

'Mind you,' her husband continued, 'most of the rest of the world won't be heartbroke.'

'So he wasn't well liked?' said Carnigan, who was not amazed by this bit of information. The storekeeper chuckled.

'Well, Sheriff, if Mad Mart Dooley was runnin' for a popularity contest, he sure as shootin' was not tryin' real hard to win!' he said. There was a flicker of amusement in his eye as he said it, and the dimples at the corners of his wife's mouth deepened.

Carnigan nodded as he walked to the door.

'Can't say I took to him much my own self,' he agreed. 'Mind you, we didn't have too long to get used to each other. I'll bring the body round the back.'

*　*　*

The back of the store was a morgue, though in the desert heat, it was clear the bodies it dealt with were best got into the ground as fast as possible. There was a heavy deal table topped with a stone slab which seemed to have been brought in out of the desert, for it was rough and jagged around the sides. Somebody had laid a lead sheet over the top of it, and together, the storekeeper and his wife got Dooley off the horse and onto the slab.

'You can leave him to me, now,' the

woman told Carnigan. 'I'm Martha Abraham. This here's my husband, Leo. Pleased to meet you, sheriff. You done the world a favour turning this one off his perch.' She jerked a thumb over her shoulder at the body on the slab.

'Watch out for Gutierrez, though. He won't be pleased at this, and he's liable to be real ornery when he's not pleased. This man's death leaves him a hand short and he's got a town war on at the moment. Him and Buchan got their horns locked to be top bull in the Flats, and the way things are at the moment, Gutierrez is already lookin' pretty sick!'

Martha looked up from her task of unbuttoning the dead man's shirt.

'He's goin' to look sicker,' she said. 'And if Buchan wins this town war, so are we. Hoffman keeps this town balanced pretty careful, just by playin' one side off agin' the other. Now there ain't no balance, and Buchan will be able to do what he wants, once Gutierrez is out of the picture.'

Carnigan leaned his hip against a tall

stool against the back wall and rolled himself a cigarette. It seemed to him that Martha had something to tell him and he needed all the information he could get.

'Just fill me in about the set-up here,' he invited her. 'I sure as shootin' ain't had all the information I need if I'm goin' to make sense of this here town.'

Martha exposed the dead man's chest, and whistled as she saw the wound.

'Nasty one!' she said. 'Leo, help me move him.'

Her husband helped her turn the dead man on his side, and they both stared at the gaping hole in his back. The bullet, as Carnigan already knew, had gone in through his chest and come out under the opposite shoulder blade, apparently breaking his spine as it passed.

The lean storekeeper stepped back and let the corpse fall back onto the table.

'Hoffman got somethin' on you?' he

asked Carnigan. The new sheriff shook his head.

'Nope. Needed eatin' money and the prospects round here didn't look too great. When he offered me the star I was pretty curious. I could be anybody or anything, so far as Hoffman knows!'

Martha went on with her job of stripping the corpse to the waist, and bandaging the wound. She did not bother with the lower half of the body.

'Tell him, Leo!' she said flatly. 'He's going to find out soon enough anyways!'

The storekeeper nodded.

'Most of the folks in this town are here because they're in debt to Hoffman, and they can't get away. We was on our way to California, like most of the pilgrims along here. But the trail is long, and there is usually Indian trouble, and there ain't no water, except in some tanks and a couple of Indian waterholes.

'We got split off from our wagon train back a ways, and just followed the trail. Time we got here, two of the oxen was dead, and the other four wasn't in good shape. We stopped outside town and I come in for supplies.'

Martha snorted. 'Supplies! He means a drink!'

Her husband shrugged. 'Have it your own way, Martha. Leastways, I did have a drink. It tasted terrible, and I left most of it, and set off for the door. Never made it.'

Martha said: 'He played cards! Lost all his money and they took the wagon and the beasts in payment. We was stuck here!'

Carnigan nodded. 'But that nice Mr Hoffman had a place for you? You could work in the general store, until you had paid off your gamblin' debt?'

Martha nodded, bitterly. 'You come across the trick before? We work all the hours God sends, but somehow there ain't ever enough money at the end of the month to both live and pay off the debt?'

'Heard about it before. Come across

it before, too. You can live, but you can't move. You run his business and he gets rich and you just get tired. Anybody else in town in the same fix?'

They nodded and exchanged smiles.

'Jenny over at Polly's eating house. Bill Brashaw the smith. Most of the businesses in town belong to Hoffman but run by people in the same fix.

'Nobody really owes him any money. You get a shot of drugged liquor and when you wake up, they tell you a tale. There's a permanent poker game goin' on at the Hoffman House, and everybody who comes in sets down to talk to Hoffman.

'Time they come to, everybody in the saloon swears they sat down and played a hand of cards — but lost. Can't prove you didn't, and them that argues with him is callin' every gunsel in the saloon a liar. Round here, life gets shorter if you call any of those bad actors liars. Real short!'

Her husband nodded. 'Try to get away and there's over a hundred miles of desert in most directions. Stay here or you get shot. Nobody likes the idea of gettin' shot.'

'Ain't too thrilled to be dry-gulched myself,' said Carnigan. 'There was two of them out there tryin' to ventilate my hide, and now I'm goin' to have to be lookin' out for the other one.'

Martha started to say something, then closed her mouth again, and turned away.

'Good luck, Sheriff,' she called, as he took the horse through to the main street. 'Stay away from dark corners.'

He waved a hand over his shoulder, and climbed onto his own horse before leading the dead man's beast down the street to the livery stable.

He told the old man there to look after the saddle, left his own horse, and carried the confiscated guns and the bandanna containing the contents of the dead man's pockets back to his office.

There, he rolled himself a cigarette, brewed some coffee on the stove and dug the package of 'Wanted' posters out of the drawer.

Mart Dooley's face stared up at him from the third one down. It was an artist's impression, and not a very good one, but it was undoubtedly Dooley, There was a reward of $500 on his head, offered by the marshal in Yuma, and he folded the paper into four and tucked it into his shirt pocket.

He already knew that Dooley had been in the town for a period, and his vanished predecessor must have known it, too. Maybe he had simply never had time to do anything about it — or maybe he had tried to do something, but somebody ran him out of town before he had a chance.

Now that he came to think of it, where exactly had the previous holder of his office gone to? All he had heard was that the unfortunate man had been run out of town on a mule. But to where? There was no railroad link closer than Tucson, and the stage line did not pass through Sidewinder Flats. Come to that, the nearest place a man could get transport was either Fort Yuma or Gila Bend.

Tucson was a possibility, of course, but for any one of those destinations, the man needed transport, and the kind of mule the local yahoos would use to run the sheriff off would hardly be a beast healthy enough to cross many miles of desert.

No, unless he had been given help, the late sheriff was still around Sidewinder Flats, and if so, it was more likely that he was under the earth than on it.

It was full dark outside, now, and the few lights outside the saloons and the general store were glowing only feebly. He blew out the lamp and let himself out of the back door rather than the front, then sidled round the building, up the alleyway, and stood in the shadows, and watched the street.

There was a good moon, and as his eyes became accustomed to the gloom, he could make out more detail of the street.

For one thing, the town was not nearly as dead as it at first appeared. Shadows occasionally flitted down its sidewalks. Doors opened and closed. There was music coming from the saloons, and the faint sound of a guitar being played down at the Mexican quarter.

In the restaurant, the lights were bright and cheerful, and he made his way there, carefully avoiding outlining himself against windows and lighted doorways.

Inside, Jenny Rennes was serving steaks and potatoes to a table full of men dressed in trail clothes and mining gear. He was reminded that there was at least one working mine within striking distance of the town, and at the single tables along the side of the room, two married couples were eating sedately. The women avoided his eye but one of the men nodded at him without speaking.

He chose the same table as that morning, put his hat on the nearby peg, and smiled at Jenny when she came along. She looked startled to see him and her face clouded.

He ordered steak and potatoes with a couple of eggs, and coffee. She brought him a cup and filled it from the big urn on the counter, and leaned over him to talk quietly.

'Are you insane?' she hissed as she filled the cup. He stared at her, surprised. She ran a glance over the room and made a play of handing him the sugar bowl and cream jug. He refused them both.

'What are you doing here? Don't you know they are out to kill you?' she asked, covering the question by fussing over the table.

He was so surprised that he could only stare at her.

'They are out all over town looking for you! Word is that Buchan's men are sure they ran you out of town this morning, and the Gutierrez gang are after you because you killed Dooley,' she said. 'I thought you had enough sense to ride on! Why are you back here?'

He shrugged and spread his hands helplessly.

'Ain't got no place else to go, ma'am!' he said. 'I am the sheriff of this place when all's been said and all's been done! I got a star and a gun and an office. Where else would I be?'

'Anywhere else! Anywhere in the world but here!' she said, angrily. 'Do you know how many sheriffs we've had since I came here? Four! Four men wore that star and four men died wearing it, that I know of for certain.'

He was staring, not at her, but past her at the door. It was being pushed open very warily. The top half was glazed with small panes, but there was a light hanging from the roof of the stoop outside, and he could see through the glass. There was nobody standing on the sidewalk, yet something was pushing the door open, and that something did not want to be seen.

'You own a dog or a cat, ma'am?' he

asked. She looked stunned.

'Have you heard a word I've said?' she snapped, forgetting the lower her voice in her irritation. 'They are out to kill you, man! You've walked into something you don't understand, here. Get out, while you can!'

He slipped the pistol out of his holster and held it, fully cocked, in his hand under the table top. The door was a good foot open, now, and it had stopped moving. To shoot in, whoever was out there would have to open it a good foot further to draw a bead through the opening.

He grabbed the woman's arm and pulled her down below the table top, ignoring her startled squeal of outrage. The two couples sitting at the tables along his side of the room jerked round, and he roared: 'Everybody down!'

Slow reactors were inclined to become dead reactors in this part of Arizona, and the entire room hit the floor as one. Through the gap between door and doorpost, he saw a spark of light, a gun roared and splinters zipped out of the wall where his head had been.

Jenny screamed in mingled shock and outrage, and one of the ranchers' wives gave a bellow of rage and grabbed for her husband's gun. The other screamed shrilly. The customers all reacted differently but they all made a similar amount of noise. It was pandemonium, and in the uproar, any chance he might have had of getting his hands on the sniper were ruined.

Two of the men ran to the door and looked out into the night, but they came back into the room shaking their heads.

'Get away from the door!' he roared at them. With the light behind them, nobody in the street could tell whose head was framed in the doorway, and both of then realised it even as he spoke.

'Sorry, Sheriff!' said one, a miner from his clothes, and added: 'He got away!'

Carrigan nodded and said: 'Thanks!' The fact was self evident, anyway.

All eyes in the room were staring at him and he correctly guessed they were waiting for him to go. He stood up and left by the rear door. It was, he thought, becoming a habit he would be glad to break.

Jenny saw him out, and caught his sleeve as he went past her.

'Come back later when the lights are out,' she said. 'If you haven't got the sense to go, then you'd better learn what you are getting yourself into. I'll have some food for you. Come after ten!'

★ ★ ★

In the event, it was later when he walked to the rear door, and tapped on the frame. She had it open immediately, and dragged him inside by his collar. Surprised and annoyed, he allowed her to, and found himself sitting in the semi dark in the kitchen. Black cloths hung

95

over the windows, and only a couple of candle lamps on the floor threw a fitful light in the room.

She sat him down at the table and brought his meal from the oven. It was beef and potatoes, and still very hot and he burned his mouth as he wolfed it down. It was the first meal he had eaten since breakfast, and he needed it.

Jenny sat at the other side of the table and he noticed that she kept herself away from the windows.

He wiped his plate with a hunk of bread and leaned back with his coffee cup in his hand.

'All right, lady,' he said. 'What's goin' on in this town?'

She ran a hand through her hair and sighed.

'What you've got here is a range war within a town, and all the nastier for that,' she said. 'Hoffman's got his tail in a crack, and his only way out is by getting himself an ally who can fight off two gangs at once, and do it without turning his back on the inhabitants!'

'Kinda hard to do,' he conceded, leaning his elbows on the table and sipping his coffee. It was cooling rapidly, and he drank deeply. The caffeine in the brew helped him keep his eyes open and he was bone tired.

'Harder with a bullet in your back,' she said bitterly. 'And that's what you are liable to get if you stay. Hoffman stays in power in this place because he has always been able to balance one side off against the other. Now, the balance has gone and you shooting Dooley has made things worse.'

'Gee, I'm sorry!' he said. 'Next time I'll just let them shoot me and die. That won't annoy anybody, will it? I sure as shootin' hate upsettin' people!'

She dropped her head into her hands and swore bitterly. He was unused to hearing a woman swear, and it jarred on him. Saloon girls could have a vocabulary which would embarrass a cavalry sergeant, but he was not used to respectable women doing the same thing.

'Don't you see, you stupid man? If you upset the balance here, one side or the other will take over. With Dooley still around, Gutierrez was as strong as Buchan. Now he's gone, Buchan can take over. There will be a gunfight like the Territory hasn't seen since the War Between The States!'

Arizona had hardly been involved in the Civil War. A spatter of fighting around Picacho Peak, a half-hearted attempt at a Confederate takeover, and then the fighting and the armed men had moved away. The Apache problems had started for exactly that reason: the Apaches saw the blue-bellies leave, and thought they had driven them out.

'And how will that affect you? With Hoffman gone, there's nothing to keep you here. You can go where you like.'

She raised her head and looked at him, and in the flickering light of the lantern he could see the desperation in her eyes.

'No,' she spat. 'No, I can't go! The only thing keeping me safe now is that one side daren't do anything because of the other side! Spoil the balance, and who is going to keep those men off me?'

The light dawned at last. He had been mildly surprised that a woman as good looking as Jenny was not attached to one man or another, but put it down to the loss of her husband.

Now, he understood what kept Hoffman alive in a land dominated by bad actors, what kept Sidewinder Flats going in a land where long life was not usually an option.

'So that's why the traders toe the line for Hoffman?' he said. 'For fear of worse.'

And it would be worse, he knew. Very much worse.

6

Garside Hoffman sat behind his table under the staircase in the Hoffman House, and seemed to be concentrating on his hand of cards. A glass of amber liquid stood at his right hand and there was a hand-rolled cigar waiting in the ashtray by his left.

Hoffman was in serious trouble and he knew it.

Sidewinder Flats had looked perfect for what he planned: a thieves' roost protected by the desert and mountains as a fort is protected by its moat and battlements. Hoffman had gone to considerable trouble to make sure that anything worth money in Sidewinder Flats belonged to him and him alone.

The former owners of the various businesses in town had been easy meat for a man who had cut his commercial teeth on war profiteering in the War

Between the States. He had started the war as a mate on a fast schooner trading out of Boston and finished as owner.

At the end of war, he was a rich man, but it was then he made a rare mistake, and left much of his money in the hands of a business associate he thought was more than just a partner, and who used it to buy herself a place in the new order.

So he made his way West and used the money he had salvaged to buy himself a freight line. The line brought him to Arizona Territory, which had not been badly touched by the war, and finally to Sidewinder Flats.

He stopped at the Flats first because his freight line needed a watering station in its way through from Fort Yuma.

Sidewinder Flats was remote from even the rough and ready law of the Territory, yet it was the only place a miner from one of the burgeoning mines out in the badlands could go to

101

get a drink, a game of cards and female companionship.

Hoffman's stock expanded as he went on. The wagons which had made it only this far were easy enough to cannibalize to make saleable whole vehicles. Teams were assembled, and Hoffman used the wagons for his freight lines and sold them further West. Men began to drift in, some with goods to sell and some merely with information, each one got a drink at Hoffman's table, and each found he had an amiable and interested ear into which to pour any news or inside information he might happen to have.

Hoffman sold the information on surprisingly cheaply. Those who could not afford to buy outright simply came to an agreement and paid him a percentage of the loot. Often, they even sold it through Hoffman's own mart, and paid a percentage on that, too. Some did not pay, but it slowly became clear that such welshers did not prosper. Indeed, an increasing number of them did not even survive.

His name spread fast, which meant that bad men, as well as their information were attracted to the little sun-baked town out on the flats, in the hope that they could do to Hoffman what Hoffman was doing to others.

They were wrong, and often fatally so. Hoffman also attracted lazy men like Tex Buchan and Antonio Gutierrez, who found if they did Hoffman's bidding, they had a place to shelter, until one of Gutierrez' men picked a fight with one of Buchan's owlhoots, and a war broke out. It was a war which was undeclared, and the more vicious for that.

Riding stock went missing from the holding pens outside the town just after either Buchan or Gutierrez had bought it. Stages were raided just before the purchasers of one of Hoffman's ready made plans could put the plans into action.

The former pirate and plotter could read the signs only too clearly: in their lust for money, the two gangs were in danger of destroying what both of them so dearly wanted. Hoffman needed a strong, dangerous ally to get rid of one or the other of the contenders for his throne, and he needed that man right away.

After two false starts, he reckoned he had found that man in Carnigan. The newcomer was clearly a tough and dangerous character, and he was on the loose with too little money and too much country to cover.

He got off to a flying start, too. Hoffman was impressed.

Hoffman was also, however, made uneasy by the speed with which Carnigan summed up the situation in town and dealt with it. He had expected lead to fly, indeed, wanted it, so long as it served his own purpose. But Carnigan was so sudden, so fast and so deadly, that an instinct deep in Hoffman's devious mind stirred and reared its head.

The death of Mart Dooley was an

unexpected event. Dooley was a practised assassin, and one with a strong sense of self-preservation, yet he had died the moment he tackled Carnigan — and tackled him from cover, to boot.

Carnigan had a gift, too, for moving around without being seen. Time after time, somebody went after him only to find that the new sheriff had disappeared, and popped up somewhere else, fast, deadly and apparently untouchable.

Hoffman needed a diversion while he sorted out his position with Carnigan, and he needed it now. The diversion came that very night, and it came well on its way to being roaring drunk.

Bandy Mack was a well-enough known character around the region. He was famous mainly for being a dirty man in a region where bathwater was almost as scarce as gold. Bandy, his matted hair hanging down to his shoulders, was so dirty that his skin was the colour of lead. He smelled spectacularly in a land where cow herders had to be cut out of their clothes at the end of a drive, and taking a bath usually meant falling off a horse into a creek. In a place where the creeks were dry most of the year, that made baths rare. Yet Bandy was famous for his filth, and there were prospectors around who swore they had seen rattlers bite Bandy, only to crawl away and die.

His main talent was that he could find drink no matter where he was or how broke, which he was most of the time.

Tonight Bandy rode into town on his scabby mule, roaring drunk and smelling if anything even worse than usual, fell through the doors of the Hoffman House, and before they could throw him out again, spilled a pile of nuggets onto the bar and declared, 'Drinks is on me, boys! I done struck it rich!'

Sidewinder Flats had a nose for riches that would have made a hungry wolf envious, and within minutes, the bar was full of local folks, every single one of them eager to help Bandy celebrate and hoping to pick up some clue which would give him a hint as to where exactly Bandy had done his striking.

The bartender had seen enough raw gold to recognize Bandy's nuggets for the real thing, and the party began to pick up speed right away.

Hoffman winced when the bartender brought the old man over to his table, and there was no need to tell the boys to make themselves scarce on this occasion — they almost trampled one another underfoot to give him room. They remained, though, within earshot. The rest of Bandy's new friends crowded round, glasses in hand, and listened carefully.

★　★　★

Bandy sat back nursing the jug he had bought at the bar, and grinned at Hoffman. In the grey of his face, his eyes were startlingly clear, bright blue irises and clean white together.

'Ain't you a-goin' to git me throwed out, Mr Hoffman?' the old man crowed, thumping his jug on the table. 'Not a-goin' to tell me to make meself scarce and stand downwind while I'm a-doin' it? Naw? Could that be on account of this here?'

He thumped a nugget on the table half the size of his fist, and even Hoffman could not conceal his wonder at the sight. It was pure gold, a rich deep yellow gold without the usual veins of quartz running through it. It sat there on the table and glowed at him and Hoffman, who was familiar with riches, felt the very beginning of the lust they called gold fever stir in his arteries.

He reached out a hand to touch it, and Bandy let him take it. The weight surprised Hoffman even though he had felt gold many a time before.

'Where did you find it, Bandy?' he asked, controlling the tremor in his voice at the very touch of so much gold.

The old man cackled like a hen.

'Wouldn't you like to know, Mr Hoffman? Wouldn't you jest love to know where ol' smelly Bandy found that there? Well, Mr Hoffman, I ain't a-goin' to tell nobody for nothin'! Not me! You can't wheedle it out o' me, you can't trick it out o' me, and you can't beat it out o' me because ol' Bandy been a prisoner o' the Apaches, and what they don' know about pain ain't been invented yet!'

Hoffman shot him a glance that had murder in it, and the startlingly blue eyes caught it and rightly interpreted it.

'Like to kill me, Mr Hoffman? Like to take ol' Bandy by the throat and choke the life out o' him? Well, you can't! Not and have the gold as well. Ain't nobody else knows where I found that, and I sure as shootin' ain't goin' to tell nobody!'

He leaned forward and Hoffman blenched at the wave of stench that came across the table at him.

'But,' said Bandy, in a whisper that could have been heard at the far side of the street, 'but I might *sell* it to somebody!'

He leaned back in his chair, rested the jug on his forearm and took a long pull from it, wiping his lips on the back of his hand when he had finished.

Hoffman raised his finger, and the barman brought him a bottle of Scotch whisky from his private store, a bottle whose label was rarely seen in the Hoffman House. It was a single malt and Hoffman had imported it personally from a small distillery on a Scottish island at enormous expense for his own private use.

He cracked the seal, took a deep breath and held it as he leaned across the table and poured a generous measure into a shot glass by Bandy's hand. The pungent aroma of the drink floated into the old prospector's nostrils and Hoffman could have sworn he saw them twitch at the smell.

'If you are going to be rich, Bandy,' he said in a deep, resonating voice which could be heard all over the room, 'you better get used to something better than that rotgut you got in that jug! Drink hearty!'

He raised his own glass and took a drink, keeping his eyes on Bandy's, and because he was watching carefully, he saw the slight flicker of the eyelids as the old man picked up the glass.

Suddenly, he knew that Bandy was not nearly as drunk as he looked and sounded. Behind those bright blue eyes — eyes which were, when he came to think about it, neither as unfocused nor as bloodshot as they should be in the state Bandy was representing — there was a working brain, and it was concentrating at the moment on him.

Bandy left the Scotch where it was on the table and raised his jug to his mouth again. Hoffman watched his throat as the old man seemed to drink and his Adam's apple bobbed only once. The jug might be at his lips but the liquor was not going down his throat.

'Well, Bandy,' said Hoffman, carefully, 'sounds like we might do some business here, maybe. Just what are you offering me, and what do you want for it? Spill it out, man!'

Bandy shook his head slowly and banged the jug down on the table.

'Not right here, Mr Hoffman,' he said. He tapped the side of his nose drunkenly with a forefinger so filthy that Hoffman could see the cracks in the dirt around the joints.

'Why not here, Bandy? You're among friends,' he said.

The blue eyes crinkled at the corners with amusement. 'Your friends, mebbe, Mr Hoffman. Not mine. We do our talkin' in private with a bottle *I* buy, and mebbe — just mebbe — we can talk us up a deal. Meanwhile,' — he grabbed up the nugget from the table and it disappeared into the arrangement of filthy rags he called clothes — 'it's drinks for the house on ol' Bandy Mack!'

He reached into his rags again, and

tossed a small leather pouch onto the bar. It hit with a solid 'clunk', and the barkeep picked it up and was turning away when Bandy shouted loudly, 'I want that weighed, so's I know there's enough to buy all my new friends a drink! And don't try sellin' me short, Jed Pritt, I know what it weighs and I know what you pay for raw gold hereabouts.'

Hoffman gave the barkeep a nod and the gold was weighed and the total announced in a loud, clear voice. Bandy shot the barkeep a long look, and grinned.

'Well, you ain't stealin' more'n an arm and a leg, Jed. OK, we'll settle for that, and you can toss in a change of clothes from Hoffman's store. These uns've got theirselves all wore out keepin' me decent!'

He stood up, suddenly more steady than he had been since he came in, and took his jug with him.

'Leo!' he called. 'Open up that there store o' Mr Hoffman's and I'll take a change from the skin outwards, and don't try passin' off no cheap goods on a poor old drunk like me.'

'We don't sell cheap clothes,' Hoffman protested automatically. Bandy gave him a long, patient look.

'Yes you do, Mr Hoffman. You just charge a lot for 'em, is all. Belly up to the bar, boys. I'll be back!'

And he was gone into the night, jug on his shoulder, before Hoffman could say anything.

Leo Abraham cocked an eyebrow at Hoffman, and the saloon owner nodded.

'Give him anything he wants,' he growled. 'Then bring him back here!' Later, he promised himself, there would be balancing of the books. But at the moment, he wanted the old prospector in a good mood.

7

Outside the door, the old prospector laid his hand on Abraham's shoulder, ignoring the storekeeper's instinctive flinch away, and began to sing something blurred in a cracked voice as they made an unsteady way across the street to the general store.

There was a light burning inside, and when Abraham knocked, his wife appeared and let them into the building. She pulled the drapes across the door when she had done it and looked agonized at the sight of Bandy making himself comfortable on a sack of beans.

'Ain't nothin' as comfy as a bag o' beans,' he said, putting down his jug on the floor. He gave a grimace as he did so. 'Pizen!' he said sadly. 'How folks kin drink this muck beats me. Jest the smell's enough to turn a man's belly.'

Abraham was stunned. 'Well, Hoffman offered you a decent glass of whiskey and you turned him down!' he protested. 'That was good Scotch, too! I get it in for him and I know what it costs.'

The old man grinned and winked at him.

'Yeah? Didn't see him takin' a drink of it his own self, though, did ye? He sat there sippin' away on that glass he keeps by his hand, all the time. You gotta ask yourself, now why would a man offer pure good Scotch to a drunken, smelly ol' desert rat, and not drink it hisself?'

Abraham stared at him, the thought dawning on him that Bandy did not sound drunk at all, now.

'Well, I'll tell you why that good and honest man, Mr Hoffman, might offer fine imported Scotch to an old desert man, and not drink it hisself. Because there was somethin' in that bottle along o' that fine old Scotch whisky, and you can jest bet your best Sunday-go-to-Meetin' boots it ain't no health tonic for the good o' drunken ol' prospectors. No sir! One good slug o' that fine Scottish likker and I'd need a place to lay me down for a long sleep and when I woke up, it'd be with my feet in a slow fire or some such.'

He winked at Martha, who was watching him from a safe distance and lifted the jug from the floor.

'You ain't got nothin' in your stock here that's better for an old man's guts than this rattler juice, have you? No? It figures. Ah, well, it ain't for much longer, I guess.'

'What are you going to do?' asked Martha, who had summed up the old man quicker than her husband.

'Do? I'm gonna sell my mine to the sidewinder o' Sidewinder Flats, and set me up a general store somewhere a good long way from here, I kin tell you! Worked out long ago that the *hombres* who make the money out of a gold strike ain't the miners who ate dust and rock for years findin' it. No sirree! It's the ones who sold them the picks and shovels, the mules and pack saddles, the bacon and beans to go find it, and then develop the strike.'

There was the sound of hands clapping slowly and loudly from the back of the store where the makeshift morgue backed onto the alleyway, and Carnigan stepped into the pool of light around the lamp.

'First time I heard a prospector talk sense about gold,' he said admiringly. 'And you sure as shootin' ain't as pickled as you look, you old gila monster.'

The old prospector spread his hands in protest.

'Me? I'm stinkin' drunk!'

Carnigan shook his head. 'Stinkin', yeah: drunk, no. That's just the way you smell. I watched you in the saloon and there wasn't a man there not tryin' to work out where you got that gold, and you never give a single hint. Takes a wily old cuss to do that in his cups, and a wily old cuss is what I'm lookin' at right now!'

The bright blue eyes measured him up and down, and the old man gave a wheezy laugh.

'Since we're talkin' kinda straight here, I'll put in two cents' worth my own self. The sheriff o' Sidewinder Flats ain't as interested in catchin' bad men as he is in findin' some horses as got stole right recent, up country a way. Am I right, sonny?'

Carnigan grinned. 'You know darned well you're right, you old goat. But talk about it any more round this town, and you and me gonna fall out, understand?'

Bandy Mack grinned and tapped the side of his nose. 'Thought I recognized you in the saloon back there. I seen you up to Placerville a couple o' times, takin' horses to the Fort. The others was too busy tryin' to get a secret out of an old drunk to notice you, but you snuck up on 'em like a Comanche with a space to fill on his scalp stick. Well, don't worry about me, sonny, I got my own problems to take up my time.'

119

The Abraham couple had been watching the exchange with bemused expressions.

'Is that right?' she said. 'Are you after stolen stock? You're not a real sheriff?'

Carnigan threw her a wink. 'I'm a rancher after my horses, Martha, but they stuck this star on me, and while I'm here, the star stays. They wanted a sheriff and now they got themselves one. Just don't get in my way.'

Martha clicked her tongue and shook her head, but from her expression she was not bothered by the news. Her eye had a more calculating look in it.

Carnigan sat down a prudent distance from Bandy Mack.

'All right, Bandy,' he said, 'what gives, now?'

The old man leaned forward and put his elbows on his knees.

'Now,' he said, 'I'm goin' to try the impossible. I'm goin' to try and sell my mine to Hoffman and survive. Wanna see how I'm gonna do it?'

Carnigan glanced through the store

window at the street. There were men standing on the sidewalk outside the Hoffman House, watching the store carefully. They had glasses in their hands, but not one of them, he thought, looked as though he was drunk.

'You better get on with whatever you're supposed to be doin',' he warned. 'They're watching the store, and they don't look too patient to me.'

The old man stirred himself from the bean bag and walked down the store, pulling shirts and jeans out of the racks, and tossing them on the counter. He added a couple of union suits and some heavy miners' boots and socks, and reached for a leather coat from the wall racks.

'You got two o' these?' he asked Abraham. The storekeeper shrugged. 'Sure!' he said in a weary voice. 'Same size?'

''Course,' the old man told him, and took one set of clothing back into the back room of the store. There was a sound of huffing and puffing, and eventually he reappeared looking at least halfway civilized. Civilized, but still dirty.

'Bandy,' protested Martha, outraged. 'At least get a wash. Putting those new clothes on a body as dirty as yours will just ruin them. And you'll still smell!'

The old prospector grinned. 'Won't last too long and I can afford a new set o' duds after all's over,' he told her. 'Tell Hoffman it is part of the price. Hey, sheriff.'

Carnigan looked up from the work of rolling a cigarette.

'Sheriff, I have to take Hoffman back to my mine so he can see it's real, and I need somebody to watch my back while I'm doin' it. You feel like comin' along? Might be useful to you to see what I got to sell.'

Might be a good way of getting rid of a witness to his play-acting, too. On the other hand, Hoffman needed watching.

'Sure, I'll come along. When you going?'

He struck a match on the seat of his

jeans, and lit the cigarette, watching the old man through the smoke.

'Daybreak, I guess. We kin get a-goin' at first light,' said Bandy Mack. His eyes flickered slightly as he said it, and Carnigan noticed the flicker and thought of the knife in his boot.

'Get started and I'll join you outside o' town,' he told the old man. 'Best the boys don't know where I've gone right off, or there'll be hell to pay soon as they find out.'

This journey promised to be more dangerous even than being the sheriff of Sidewinder Flats, and that was saying something.

With that thought in his mind, he loaded the sixth chamber of the Colt when he got back to his office, and checked the action on his Winchester. After a moment's thought, he slipped the pistol he had taken from Dooley behind his belt buckle with the butt turned to the right.

Then he took his bedroll and canteen and a bait of food in his saddle-bags and slipped out of the rear door of the jail to collect his horse from the stable.

He camped in a different fold of ground from the previous nights, picketed his horse nearby, and drank cold water and ate jerky before he turned in.

The night was cold and clear, and the desert under a canopy of stars seemed to have been silver plated with the shadows picked out in ebony. The horse ate the feed he had brought for it, drank from his hat and stood, hipshot and head down, as he slept.

The night was silent save for the sounds of the creatures of the dark, and they avoided the smell of man and went about their business without disturbing him.

★　★　★

He was awake before first light, boiling water for coffee over a capful of fire, and chewing on campfire bread and bacon. From his position in the rocks above the trail he could see down onto the road and he saw the old prospector and his pack horse emerge and start down the road.

With him was a buckboard which contained a squat figure which could only be Hoffman, and a driver Carnigan recognized as Jed, the barman from the Hoffman House. There was nobody else in the party, but as he watched the men start down the road, a number of figures straggled, one by one, from the outskirts of the town and started after them.

Carnigan climbed into the saddle and kept pace with what was quickly turning into a procession.

★   ★   ★

The old prospector led the buckboard along the trail at an easy, relaxed pace, and the trailing hopefuls tagged along behind, the ones in front slowing down to avoid overtaking the buckboard, and the ones behind inevitably catching up on the leaders.

Twice he started to angle his trail down the hillside to join the old prospector and Hoffman, and twice his instincts warned him to stay clear of them, so he returned to the faint trail.

He was just about to make his third attempt to ride down to the road and join the old miner and Hoffman when he saw the first mist of dust in the air ahead, and knew instantly that his instinct had been right, and they were riding into danger.

No wonder he had not been able to locate the source of his unease — it was ahead of them, not behind.

So did old Bandy Mack know what was out there, waiting for them? Or was he, too, riding into danger unaware of it?

Unlikely, thought Carnigan. Bandy was as wily as a sackful of monkeys, and he knew the land better than anybody else around. He was leading the inevitable followers into an ambush, which would get them off his tail.

So how did he hope to avoid the trap himself? Or did he indeed hope of evade it?

Carnigan examined his own back trail again, but there was still no sign of dust and out in this desert, it was impossible to move without raising dust. The threat was up ahead, and Bandy knew about it.

He was just putting over his reins to ride down to warn the townsmen what was waiting for them up ahead when he realized that he could no longer see Bandy and Hoffman on the road.

Between him and the trail there were a couple of massive outcrops of rock, with their shoulders buried in the steep side of the mountain and he had assumed without thinking about it that the buckboard was passing behind one of them, but by now it should have reappeared, and it had not.

Ambushed? There had been no shooting, and from up here, he should have been able to catch any high-pitched war cries. So whatever had happened had happened in silence.

Or, he reminded himself, Bandy had dropped into hiding to avoid the waiting ambush, and was down there, somewhere behind that near spike of rock.

As he guided the horse down the hillside, he heard the first spatter of shooting below, and the group of townsmen broke into turmoil. The ambush had already been sprung, and Hoffman was already getting away.

8

The Apaches had timed their ambush beautifully, except for the fact that they expected to be tackling a bunch of unsuspecting farmers and miners and what they caught was a gang of trigger-happy outlaws.

For the moment, Gutierrez and Buchan had put aside their differences in favour of their lust for gold, and they were on edge and wary to be riding with their former enemies. Hands were resting on guns, ears were pricked for the faintest hint of trouble and nerves were tense as bowstrings.

At the first shot, the party hit the ground. One or two were successful in pulling their horses down with them and using the animals as ramparts. The other mounts, spooked, ran for it. But they were used to gunfire, and they did not run far.

That first shot hit Marshall, one of Buchan's men; it hit his cartridge belt and exploded a couple of the shells there. The wound on his hip was messy and painful, but it was not disabling. Marshall made it to the cover of a rock at the side of the road, swearing luridly, and began firing back at his attackers immediately.

The Apaches found the ambush more than they had expected. What they had thought was to be a short, bloody slaughter of white men for their horses, their equipment and for pure devilry was turning into a stand-off, and, being a pragmatic people, before long the warriors withdrew to fight another day.

Within minutes, the firing had first reduced from a storm to a spatter and finally stopped altogether for lack of targets. Marshall's wound was the only damage sustained by the white men, and there were no blood spots in the rocks to indicate Apache victims.

'Damned Injuns!' snarled Marshall,

as somebody swabbed out his wound with water from his canteen and dabbed a couple of brass fragments out of the bloody mess.

The men who were still mounted rounded up the horses which had run off and brought them back to the group and, after some discussion, the party set off again, going more cautiously and keeping a sharp eye open for a return of the Apaches.

Carnigan watched the battle from his vantage point higher on the hillside, and was relieved to see the Apaches filtering away in the opposite direction, towards the open desert.

What did interest him was where the old prospector and the buckboard containing Hoffman and his bartender, Pritt, had gone. He remained where he was, watching the party from town assembling themselves and resuming its pursuit.

Like the buckboard and the old man, they disappeared behind the great spike of rock along the trail. Unlike them, the party later reappeared on the far side, and carried on along the trail.

It would have taken a really expert tracker to find the buggy's wheel tracks even if they had been there, he knew. This was the trail taken by Hoffman's wagons on their way up country towards Tucson and Phoenix, and it was rutted with wagon tracks.

He waited until the party had disappeared along the road, then made his cautious way down from the hillside. Just because he had seen the Apaches ride away from their ambush site, did not mean that there might not be another party, or even a single scout.

He picked up the wagon tracks as soon as he hit the trail, clean and recent among the older ruts, and followed them warily under the face of the rock sentinel on the uphill side of the trail. There was a maze of tangled tracks there where a stretch of boulder-strewn ground forced the trail further under the face of the pinnacle. He found the cleaner ruts made by the buckboard

— and almost instantly lost them again.

Frowning, he stepped down from the saddle and hunkered on his haunches by the road. The wagon tracks were there, all right, clear and crisp.

And then they were not.

He was straightening up when it struck him that the road where the tracks stopped was also suspiciously smooth. The old, deep wheel tracks, which had been hardened by the heat, were still there, but more recent ones had disappeared, as though they had been blown away.

He swore bitterly to himself, and took off his hat to waft the dusty surface of the road. As he did so, it shifted and underneath the scattering of loose dust, the deeper tracks of the buckboard were revealed.

Somebody — the wily old prospector most likely — had scattered dust over the tracks and filled them in. Likely, the old boy had also trailed a blanket over the tracks leaving the old, deeper, tracks visible but masking the more recent ones. It might have worked well enough with horse tracks, but with the buckboard, which had narrow, sharper profiles, the underlying marks in the trail remained under the loose dust.

He followed the masked trail, wafting the dust with his hat, and revealing the point where the buckboard had pulled aside from the road, making a sharp, almost right-angled turn, and run inwards towards the base of the rock. The trail led up to the apparently flat face of the huge slab, and he would have abandoned the search if he had not had the iron tyre tracks to follow. They went straight up to the rock face and stopped.

He leaned from the saddle and examined the face of the rock, finding that instead of a flat, solid cliff, he was examining a rock folded and striated like a hanging curtain.

He climbed down from the horse, looped the reins over his wrist, and examined the cliff face carefully.

Sure enough, there was a gap

between one of the outward folds of rock and the face of the great mesa itself. Inside the tunnel formed by the gap, he could see the buckboard's tracks resuming.

The tunnel climbed, gently at first and then more steeply. The light got stronger and he could hear, above him, the very faint 'tock-tock-tock' of somebody digging with a pickaxe.

He emerged from the tunnel and found himself looking into a natural amphitheatre in the centre of the mesa, like a cavity in a rotten tooth. There was vegetation in the bottom of the hole, and the sound of falling water down there, as well.

A little further and he was looking down into a natural valley almost circular in formation, and bordered with trees. At the foot of the far wall, where the mesa became part of the mountain wall, a small waterfall emerged from the cliff and dropped into a catchment pool a few yards across.

Near it was a patch of grass, and

cropping at the grass were Bandy Mack's mule and the horse which had drawn the buckboard. At the far side of the pool, almost hidden by the curtain of falling water, he could see a hole in the cliff-side.

There was no sign of Bandy, Hoffman or the bartender, but from where he stood he could still hear the sound of the pick: it was coming from the cave.

More wary than ever, he ground hitched the horse and made his way down through the stunted trees to the green patch by the pool. The animals noticed him and raised their heads to watch his progress, then dropped them again to resume eating grass.

Carefully, he angled across the little open space, and approached the cave mouth. The sound of digging was louder here, and he was puzzled that Bandy should be bothering to mine when he had a deal set up to sell the place.

As he entered the mouth of the cave,

however, he could hear voices. He leaned closer to listen.

'Deep enough, yet?' It was Bandy's voice, and he sounded sullen and angry.

There was a reply too muffled for Carnigan to hear, and a low laugh, and then the digging began again.

Carnigan eased his way into the cave mouth, down a rough passage-way within, and flattened himself against the wall. There was a glow from deeper into the cave, and against it he could see two heads outlined. From the look of them they belonged to Hoffman and Pritt.

'Keep goin'!' It was the bartender's voice, and there was an ugly note to it.

Then Bandy spoke. His voice was hoarse and sounded hopeless.

'Why kill me?' he asked huskily. 'You got the mine, now. There's gold a-plenty in here for both o' you, and the price I'm askin' ain't but a peck compared to what you'll get out of it, Mr Hoffman. What do you get outa killin' me?'

Hoffman's chuckle had an unpleasantly fat edge to it. It was the laugh of a man who had got everything he wanted, and cared nothing for the people from whom he had taken it.

'What do I get out of it, Bandy? I get gold and I get silence. Both of 'em yours, you old fool.'

'But you get both even with me alive. Why kill me?' By leaning forward, Carnigan could see into the pool of light thrown by a torch which had been jammed behind a boulder against the far wall.

In the middle of the cave, Bandy Mack was standing waist deep in an oblong hole which was plainly going to be his grave. The floor of what looked like a fair sized cavern had been filled over the years by small stones and debris from the roof and the various rock falls had exposed, deep in the rock, a seam of gold which even in the flickering light of the torch looked like molten metal flowing down the wall.

Carnigan pursed his lips in a silent

whistle at the sight. He had heard of gold strikes as rich as bank vaults but he had never seen anything as rich and apparently pure as this one.

The vein was like a thick river of metal running down the wall from somewhere up beyond the light of the torch down into the floor. As the torchlight wavered and jumped, the metal looked as though it were actually flowing.

Pritt was leaning against a boulder to Carnigan's left. He had a shotgun over his arm like a man going out for a day's shooting, and he was smoking a thin cigar. The smoke from the burning tip rose in a straight, unbroken column into the still air, showing that there was no draught running through the cavern.

Carnigan had worked in mines and was used to being underground, but he felt uncomfortable inside the belly of this hill, unable to ignore the weight of rock suspended over his head. The idea that there was no other way out of the cavern than the narrow passage through which he entered also made him jumpy. But it was nothing compared to the spasm of nerves he felt when, deep inside the rocks, there was a gentle, deep moan like an animal in pain, which went on for several seconds.

When it had stopped, a sprinkling of dust filtered down into the light of the torch like a tiny snow shower. Both Hoffman and the bartender snapped upright like rabbits at the sound of a hunting wolf, and stared wildly around them.

'What in the name o' all that's holy was that?' said Pritt, eventually. His voice had changed from its previous, confident brutality to a nervous rasp.

Bandy Mack shot him a glance from under dust-filled eyebrows.

'What was that? Why, that was the old Spaniard, a-moanin' in his grave on account of his gold's bein' stole!' he said in an amused voice. 'You never heard o' the Lost Spaniard gold mine, mister?'

Pritt scoffed, but Hoffman was

surprisingly interested. 'Go on,' he said.

'Seems that when the old Spaniards was openin' up this here territory, they was after gold,' Bandy said. 'Spanish always was after gold. They even thought there was seven cities of gold up here somewheres, because they kept seein' Indians wearin' gold ornaments and such. Thought they had to have secret mines they took the gold out of.'

He looked over at the barkeep. 'Jed, kin I have a drink from your canteen? There's a-plenty o' water outside, and this dust is gettin' to me down in this hole.'

Pritt seemed inclined to refuse, but Hoffman's attention had been caught by the tale and he reached out, picked up the canteen by its strap and swung it into the hole. Bandy caught it, and poured some water down his throat

'Well, at one time, all o' this land here was owned by the Spaniards and they used to come up from Mexico and plunder it and take Indians as slaves, and all that. They heard o' these cities

141

which was supposed to be built out o' pure gold, and they was hot as hell to find 'em. After all, they got fortunes in gold out o' the Indians down in Mexico, so why not here?'

He drank from the canteen again, and spat on the ground.

'Only there ain't no cities o' gold, and there ain't no Eldorado in Arizona. Just sand and rock and Indians.'

Hoffman spat a crumb of tobacco from the end of his cigar and stared at it, irritably. 'Get on with it!'

'Right away. But you know where I got the map brought me to this mine? Right in your bar, I got it.'

Hoffman and the barkeep stared at one another then back at the old man.

'Mr bar?' said Hoffman, surprised. 'What were you doing in my bar?'

'Gettin' drunk, what else?' said the old man. Carnigan noticed he moved constantly, reversing the shovel, moving his feet, wiping his brow with what looked like the filthiest bandanna in Arizona Territory. Each move brought him slightly closer to the Pritt and his shotgun.

But the 'keep was as careful as he was nervous. He noticed the old man's movement, and suddenly straightened up, jerking the gun off the boulder in front of him and pointing it at the old man's head.

'Keep diggin', you old sidewinder!' he snarled. His nerves were still frayed by the noises inside the mountain, but the effect was to make him more jumpy, not less.

Bandy angled a snaggle-tooth grin at him and turned back to his digging. It was a slow job because most of what he was shifting was stone chips rather than soil, and he could only move a few at a time.

Even so, he had been labouring for fifteen minutes or more when the odd rumble started again inside the mountain. This time, Pritt shot upright, and even in the flickering light of the torch, Carnigan could see he was sweating profusely.

The man glared around as the noise once again faded into silence, then pushed the shotgun towards Hoffman.

'That's deep enough!' he rasped. 'Put down the shovel! Say your prayers, you dirty old devil, and say 'em quick!'

Carnigan heard the hammers click back on the shotgun, and stood up from his hiding place, cocking his Winchester. The double click was deafening in the sudden silence in the cave, and it was followed by another groan within the rocks, this time louder and more prolonged.

Bandy Mack, to his amazement, shouted, 'No, Sheriff! Don't shoot! Don't shoot! You'll kill us all! She's just about ready to go!'

Carnigan paused, rifle halfway to his shoulder, and Pritt spun round with the shotgun in his hands. In turning, he caught Hoffman, who was sitting between him and Carnigan, a glancing blow to the shoulder, and the saloon keeper slipped off the rock and fell into the crude grave. The shotgun went off, though where the charge went, it was impossible to say. Hoffman was struggling out when the rumble from inside the rock started again and this time did not stop.

Stones and sand began to rain down from the roof and Hoffman, as he clambered out of the hole, grabbed at Pritt for support and pulled him into the grave. The man dropped the shotgun as he fell, but he was not badly hurt, and began to scramble out again, reaching for the weapon.

Bandy Mack threw himself out of the hole and began to run across the rocks towards Carnigan.

Hoffman was already shouldering past them both, going fast for a fat man, and making for the passageway to the outside world. Carnigan followed him and Bandy Mack was clawing at his back as he went.

'She's goin' to go!' the old man kept yelling. 'She's goin' to go! Get out o' my way, damn you!'

The three of them racketed along the

passageway to the outside world, colliding with each other, and stumbling on the broken stones of the path. Behind them, the roof started to rain into the cavern.

9

Somewhere along the way, Jed Pritt, the barkeep, disappeared. Carnigan didn't hear or see him go, but when the other three men got out into the hidden valley, there was a plume of dust coming out of the cave and nothing else.

Hoffman, who, despite his bulk, moved nimbly enough when his hide was threatened, stared at the dust cloud for a few moments, then shrugged and turned away. He made for his buckboard, slapping dust from his clothes as he went.

Carnigan looked at Bandy Mack and was surprised to see the old man had a shotgun in his hands. Where it had come from, he did not know, but the old man had gone nowhere near his mule, which was now cropping at the sparse grass around the water-hole.

Hoffman reached the buckboard, still slapping at his clothes, then leaned forward to reach under the seat.

'When you turn round, Hoff, there better be nothin' in your hands but air, or you are goin' to be shorter by a head!' said Bandy, in a voice that seemed to have been hewn out of the rock. Carnigan did not doubt for a moment that he meant every syllable, and neither, apparently, did Hoffman. He turned slowly, hands held away from his body and with their palms towards the old miner.

'I got no weapon!' he protested. 'I'm no threat to you, Bandy!'

'Yeah? What was you goin' to bury me in the mine for? Civic pride? Good luck? Save me from the rheumatics in my old age? You keep your hands where I kin see 'em, and don't do so much as breathe funny, or I'll blow a hole in you big enough to drive a stage through.'

Hoffman became a statue. Carnigan had been at the open end of a shotgun more than once, and he knew from experience that the barrels looked as big as railroad tunnels from Hoffman's point of view.

Bandy Mack motioned the saloon owner away from the buckboard and made him lie on his face on the ground, arms stretched above his head. When Carnigan began to move, he switched the shotgun towards him. Carnigan froze.

'Just stay where you are right this minute, Sheriff! I'm grateful for the help, but I expected you a hell of a sight earlier! Where you been all mornin'?'

Carnigan motioned with his head towards the passage from the outside world.

'Back there, followin' you. Like half the population of Sidewinder Flats was doing,' he said.

'They was? Figured we wasn't alone out there. That's why I brushed over the tracks. How come you found 'em? You see us come in here?'

Carnigan shook his head. 'Saw you ride in behind the mesa one side, and didn't come out the other,' he said. 'Short o' flyin' there was only one place you could've gone — in here. It was just a matter o' findin' the tracks, and followin' on.'

Bandy nodded. 'I forgot you was that good on the trail,' he said. 'Should've been more careful. So how many follered us from the Flats?'

'About a dozen, dozen and a half.'

'And where'd they go?'

'Got ambushed by Apaches, fought 'em off and carried on lookin' for your trail. Last I saw they were still travellin' north, a mite east. They could be nearly at the Gila by nightfall.'

'Could you see who they was? And if you move one more inch, Hoff, I swear to God I'll shorten you by a head, and you better believe it!'

The saloon owner froze again. The shotgun muzzle was back fixed in his direction, and his attempts to crawl towards the wagon were not getting him very far, anyway.

'Carny! Set yourself down and keep

your hands away from your guns. I don't want to shoot you, but if I have to, I will.'

Carnigan sat down on a rock, and put hands down in his lap. He did not doubt for a second that the old man would shoot him if he felt it necessary, though he was also pretty certain he could beat Bandy to the shot. In his lap, his hand was only a couple of inches from the butt of the pistol he had pushed behind his belt buckle.

The shotgun barrels swung away from him, and covered the prone Hoffman again. Bandy started to make his way to the buckboard, and Carnigan saw Hoffman's muscles tense, though the man remained prone.

The miner reached under the buckboard seat and slid aside the panel there. Hoffman's neck bulged and started to turn red with the strain of keeping himself prone while the man he had planned to murder fished around in the space under the seat.

Bandy gave a grunt, and pulled his

hand out of the compartment. He was holding a rawhide sack which was obviously heavy from the way he held it, and gave out a dull chink as he set it down. Hoffman was quivering with tension, and the old man looked over at him as he pulled open the neck of the sack. He had to do it one-handed as he did not want to put down the shotgun, and he was clumsy at it.

'Keep still!' he ordered again, and plunged his hand into the sack. As he did so, Hoffman rolled over, again and again. The shotgun blasted deafeningly, but the charge hit the ground where he had been, and the two rolls had taken him out of the area of the charge. Earth and small stones flew in the air, and Hoffman went on rolling behind one of the rocks that littered the basin's base.

Carnigan dropped backwards off his rock, pulling the pistol from his waistband, and rolling immediately to peer round the base of the rock on the opposite side from where he had fallen.

Bandy was already on his mule, and

the animal was galloping at a surprising speed for the exit from the hidden valley. The old prospector was hanging on the far side of the mule from Hoffman, like an Indian warrior. A wise move, since the saloon owner popped up from behind his rock with a gun in his hand and started blasting away as the mule receded towards the tunnel.

The gun he was using though, was a short-barrelled Colt designed for peace officers in towns, and though it was deadly in the confines of a saloon or a town alleyway, at any longer range it was inclined to be inaccurate, and so it proved on this occasion. The mule with Bandy now safely astride it, galloped up the slope to the exit tunnel and vanished into the entrance.

Hoffman swore foully and made for the buckboard, and Carnigan stood up and whistled for his horse. The animal, which had been drinking from the pool until the shooting disturbed it, trotted over to him.

The saloon keeper was looking for

something in the box under the seat, and he came out of it and turned towards Carnigan with a rifle in his hands. He stopped suddenly when he found himself looking into the muzzle of Carnigan's Winchester.

'No!' said Carnigan harshly. 'Drop it!'

Hoffman's eyes were slits of hatred.

'And where the hell were you when that old bastard tried to kill me?'

'Same place as I was when you was makin' him dig his own grave,' Carnigan told him. 'I was sittin' and listenin'. Heard some interestin' stuff, too.'

The saloon keeper straightened up slowly.

'I thought I told you to drop that,' said Carnigan. 'Do it now!'

For a moment he thought Hoffman was going to chance it, but the man had not become a criminal mastermind by being stupid, and he put the rifle down slowly and backed away from it.

'Better,' Carnigan said, coolly. 'What

did he get away with?'

'Gold,' said Hoffman savagely, but the heat was fading from his eyes and being replaced by calculation. 'A lot of gold. You're the sheriff, what you goin' to do about it?'

Carnigan shrugged. 'I got no jurisdiction outside of town. What can I do? He held me up same as you. You saw him.'

Hoffman's eyes were flat as a rattlesnake's. Carnigan could see him pulling himself together — and doing it mighty fast for a businessman who had just escaped death twice.

'Was that the money you showed him to make him think you were buyin' his mine?'

The gambler shot him a glance. 'What do you know about it?'

'Not much. He told me he was fixin' to sell you his strike, and seems to me that's exactly what he was doin'. Good lode, an' all, from what I could see. You should be grateful he wasn't a good shot with that scattergun, or he'd've cut you in half.'

The cold, rattlesnake eyes hooded and the fat cheeks creased into a smile that was as false as a wedding dress on a skeleton.

'You're right, of course,' the fat man told him. 'I was just upset at losing the money. That old man cost me a deal o' cash, and I was mad at him.'

'Yeah? How much?'

But Hoffman was back in command of himself, and the hooded eyes gave nothing away.

'A lot!' he said, tersely. 'Now I got a business to run. I have to get back to the Flats. You coming?'

'Sure am.' Carnigan threw a leg over his horse and was astride the saddle, with the rifle pointing straight at Hoffman's face so fast that the saloon owner was taken by surprise. He put the rifle down by the buckboard seat and climbed up himself. Once again, Carnigan noted that for a man of his bulk, he moved smoothly and easily.

'Lead on!' Hoffman said, shaking out

the lines in his hands, but Carnigan shook his head.

'Not meanin' to be disrespectful, mister, but I'd feel a deal safer if you and your Winchester was in front of me, where I can see the both of you. You lead on.'

The saloon keeper shook out the reins and clucked at the horses. The wagon wheels ratted and the buckboard ran up the slope to the entrance and disappeared into it. By the time Carnigan had emerged from the tunnel, Hoffman's wagon was already running down the slope to the trail.

Carnigan studied the country. There was no sign of the party from the Flats along the thin line of the road which led north towards Gila Bend, and the road south towards Sidewinder Flats was empty now. A dust devil whirled over the flat land towards the next line of mountains to the south-west, a leaping, weaving column of sand which stood out against the rocks of the mountains. Otherwise the countryside was empty of life and movement.

The buckboard was rattling along the trail now, but he let Hoffman have the road to himself and climbed the side of the hills back to the eyebrow trail he had followed to get here. From it, he could see the trail for a considerable distance and the buckboard and its trailing column of dust was easily visible. Hoffman was making good time back towards the town, though he was advertising his progress.

Carnigan was wondering what had happened to the Apaches. Granted their ambush had failed, but it was unlike them to have abandoned a good plan as easily. They had apparently taken no casualties, not even a flesh wound, and yet at the first return of fire, they had turned tail and run for it.

He looked for tracks as he went along the higher trail, but he did not really expect to find any, and he did not. The Indians had made a good plan, and had the sense to abandon it when they saw it had failed, and he did not blame them.

Carnigan had more reason than most to know the Apaches. At one time, he had taken an Apache wife and lived with her in her village. The life was a hard, brutal one, but he had come to respect the Indians for their ingenuity in gouging a living out of the most unforgiving country on earth.

All that had come to an end when scalp hunters hit the village while he was out hunting with the men of the community. There were no survivors, and Carnigan's wife and their baby were among the bodies strewn around burned out frames of the wickiups. He had joined the pursuit of the scalp hunters, but they were too long gone, and when the other warriors returned to bury their dead he went with them, observed the necessary rites for his own family, and then turned his back on the life and went his way.

The result of his life among the Apache was a deepened understanding of what he considered the toughest people in the world and a healthy respect for their prowess as fighting men. And the fighting men he had lived amongst would not have abandoned an ambush at the first spatter of returned fire. If an Apache left a fire fight it was because he was disabled, dead — or had something better to do.

What had these Apaches suddenly found that was better to do than a spirited fire fight with white men?

Carnigan turned his horse towards the site of the ambush, and dropped to the ground to examine the Apaches' positions.

There was, as he expected, little for him to read on the ground. He could see the positions the warriors had occupied and there was, as he had expected, no blood spot to show an injury. He found the prints of the unshod hoofs where the warriors had left their ponies during the fight.

The tracks were hard to follow through the sand and rocks, but a scrape here and an overturned stone there did give him a rough indication of the route they had followed. It led steadily northwards, keeping parallel with the road but staying on the higher ground.

From which, of course, the Indians could keep the white men they were trailing in sight. The ambush in fact was not over — merely postponed.

He urged the horse up onto the crest of the ridge where a sharp boulder broke the skyline, and concealed him while he raked the road northwards with his field-glasses.

Along the trail to the north, nothing moved.

10

Uneasily, Carnigan turned away from the ridge and began to make his way back towards Sidewinder Flats. The desert behind him looked empty enough and clear, but he felt uncomfortable. Something was not right up there, and the fact that he could actually see nothing wrong did not reassure him.

He could no longer see Hoffman in his buckboard, but he had no intention of following the fat man along the known trail, anyway. A good shot could pick off a rider almost anywhere along the route from the cover of a pile of boulders or a stand of cactus. The saguaros along the slopes were almost as thick as trees in a forest, and it took little to hide a man with a rifle.

All the same, he had the itch between his shoulder blades which desperately needed a scratch and eventually he turned the horse aside from the trail, rode back to the point above the hollow mesa, dismounted and climbed on foot to a high point on the ridge.

He was now a little behind the big mesa and slightly above it. He could see a long distance to the north, where the road disappeared into the wobbling heat-haze.

Nothing. Not a speck on the road, not a hint of dust in the air, not even a circling turkey buzzard. Just the desert, with the road etched faintly upon it, and the evenly spaced blotches of green which were the saguaros and the scrubby yuccas and ocotillos.

He lowered the glasses, and blinked his eyes to clear them, then raised them again and swept the road to the south.

Nothing.

But there should have been something. At the very least he should still be able to see, just faintly in the distance, the plume of dust from Hoffman's rig. Yet there was nothing.

He was just clearing his eyes again to do another sweep, when he heard, just above the threshold of hearing, a very faint moan.

The hairs on the back of his neck prickled and he dropped to the ground, behind a rock.

The sound came again, along with a scrabbling sound, and this time he got the direction. It came from downhill, on the same side as the road. He raised himself carefully to look around, and heard a third moan, this time more distinctly.

His first thought was a hurt animal, but he could see nothing on the exposed stretch of hillside below him. In any case, he could think of no animal which might be making such a sound.

Except, he realized, a man. A hurt man.

He rose and, crouching, slipped down the hill a way in time to hear the moan come again, along with more prolonged scratching. It was coming from the ground where a blunt tooth of rock stuck up out of the hillside. As he watched, the rock shifted slightly, and the moan came again.

He walked down the hillside, leading his horse, until he could see down the side of the boulder. There was a crack, maybe an inch wide, down the side of the rock on the uphill face. As he bent to look into it, he heard the moan again, this time quite clearly, and he could hear the sound of scrabbling coming from the crack. The rock shifted very slightly.

He leaned forward and tapped on the side of the rock. The scrabbling stopped immediately, and there was silence. Then: 'Who's there?' came up from the crack.

Carnigan sat back on his haunches and stared at the little gap. He could see dust filtering down into it from when the rock had moved, and he heard quite distinctly the man underneath coughing and spitting it out.

'Who's there? Who's out there? Help me!'

'Yeah, I can hear you, but if you don't stop shiftin' this rock, that's the last we're ever goin' to hear from you! How much room you got down there?'

A cackle of laughter with the edge of hysteria in it came out of the hole.

'Room? I got room enough to put the goddam' San Xavier Mission in, towers an' all! Mister, you better believe it, I got nothin' down here *but* room! You wanna come down and see?'

'Not much. I'd rather stay uphill of this rock you keep tryin' to undermine. You got somethin' to stand on out of the way of it?'

There was a startled exclamation, and the sound of scrabbling. The rock moved again, slightly, then in one slow and almost stately movement, it rolled out of its socket and slid away down the hillside.

From below there was a yell and a stream of oaths, but they did not diminish, and when he leaned forward and stared down through the hole left by the boulder, he could see a hand clinging to the side of the hole where the rock had been.

He ran back to his horse, shook out his rope and tied one end to the saddle horn. Then he let himself down the hillside until he was standing above the hole. There were two hands clinging to the side of the hole now, their knuckles bloodied and filthy. He put one foot in the loop, let himself down next to the hands, until he was on a level with them, and reached out to wind one arm round the chest of the man who was desperately hanging from his fingertips.

As he grabbed, the man lost his own grip on the side of the hole and almost slipped from Carnigan's grip. If he had not had his foot in the loop, the weight would have pulled him down into the gaping hole where the rock had been.

As it was, he felt as though his arms were being wrenched out of their sockets. He whistled at the horse, and slowly, they began to rise in the hole until he could get his own head above ground level. The horse was standing uphill of him, its front legs braced, holding against the strain on the rope.

'Climb up over me!' he told the man. The climber managed to get first one arm and then the other round his neck, which at least left his arms free. Within moments, the horse backed far enough up the slope for them to take their own weight, and scramble out of the hole.

The rescued man was Jed Pritt, and he was a mess. Covered in dust and dirt, half his clothes ripped away and his exposed flesh gouged and scraped, he collapsed onto the hillside, panting and gasping hoarsely, and lay on his back for a few minutes, eyes closed and mouth gaping.

'You and me has had our differences, Sheriff,' he said, when his chest had stopped heaving, 'but you sure saved a lost soul this day! Anything you want I can do, you got it!'

'I'll settle for the first drink free tonight,' Carnigan told him tersely. 'And some information about your boss.'

Pritt's expression turned foxy immediately. 'I thought you was dead, Sheriff,' he said evasively.

'And I thought you was gone for sure,' Carnigan told him equably. 'Let's say it was a miracle, on account of our pure and decent lives, and leave the rest to the good Lord! Now, what was you and Hoffman goin' to do with that old prospector, once you found his gold mine?'

Pritt started to sit up, than fell into a fit of coughing which kept him on his back for a while. Carnigan rolled a cigarette while he waited and, when he had finished, Carnigan repeated, 'What was you and Hoffman goin' to do with that old prospector, once you'd found his gold mine?'

Pritt gave him a bitter look.

'Don't you never give up?' he snarled.

'No, I never do,' Carnigan told him. 'Not while they're alive anyways, and I'm workin' on the dead right now!'

The barman leaned forward and

started to pat his clothes clear of some of the dust. It came off in clouds, but when he had finished his clothes did not look very different.

'Old Bandy been goin' off at the mouth 'bout this here Lost Spanisher Gold Mine long as I can remember. He gets his supplies in the nearest town to the stretch he's workin', puts it on the back o' that old mule, and goes off into the badlands to take up where he left off.'

'So he's got a method, then?'

'He's sure got somethin'. He comes into Hoffman's 'bout every six months or so. Has been last couple of years, anyways. He always has enough money for one good drunk, and the supplies for his next trip. Then he sleeps off the drunk, and the next mornin' he's gone again. Nobody sees him go. I've tried a few times, but I never seen him. One minute he's there, snorin' like a hawg in muck, next he's gone and his mule with him!'

That sounded like a canny old man

who enjoyed a drink and had the sense to stay clear of a real session. No genuine drunk could pull the same trick so many times without at least one person seeing him. Particularly if they thought he had made a strike.

And yet this shrewd old man, after searching his whole life for the big one, was prepared to sell it to a saloon owner he must be fully aware was more likely to steal than buy his claim.

He thought back to the scene in the cave, while Bandy was digging what was supposed to be his own grave. In his mind's eye, he could see the thick, rich seam of gold running down the far wall of the cave as though it were alive.

Open and inviting. Gold, there for the taking. Yet an old man who had devoted his entire life to finding the lode was willing to sell it off to a saloon owner he knew to be shrewd, unscrupulous, and a murderer? Hogwash! Bandy Mack had sold his soul for that gold. Nothing on earth would persuade him to part with it now he had found it.

Unless, of course, he knew that any attempt to take it out of the ground would bring the roof down on his head. He recalled Bandy's reluctance to use a pick to dig the hole his enemies intended to bury him in, the old man's panic-stricken shout, 'Sheriff! Don't shoot!' when he stood up from behind his boulder. The desperate rabbit speed with which the man leapt for the exit to the cave once the roof had started its collapse.

He knew. Crafty Old Bandy Mack knew the roof of the gold cavern was ready to come down at any time! No wonder he had been willing to take the terrible risk of being murdered and showed the hidden mine to Hoffman. It was his only way of turning the find of a lifetime into solid money.

The only thing that he had got wrong was the state of that unstable roof. It must have been closer to collapse than he had calculated, for one shot to bring the whole thing down round their ears.

While he had been working this out,

he never took his eyes from the barman, and he could see the man was puzzled by his absent-mindedness.

'How much did Hoffman have in that bag?' he asked.

Pritt looked evasive and shrugged. 'How would I know? I just keep bar for him.'

'And hold the shotgun on an old man diggin' his own grave, drive Hoffman's buggy and want to get on with killin' the old fellow: how much?'

There was a sullen moment of silence, but Pritt had been too close to death not to be aware just how thin was the division between it and survival.

'Five thousand!' he said eventually. 'The old bastard didn't know what that strike was worth! I could see more'n that stickin' out o' the wall already, and that seam wasn't nowhere near runnin' out.'

That was true, but Pritt was overlooking the fact that the old prospector knew the seam was flawed and about to collapse. Nothing else would explain his extreme panic when he thought Carnigan might fire his gun inside the mine.

After all, it only took the discharge of one barrel of the shotgun to start the collapse of the entire roof. Bandy had known what would happen, because once the gun went off, he had been out of the hole and running like a sprinter to the entrance tunnel and, once out of the hole, he showed no sign at all of going back in.

The old man had known about the state of the mine, all right. And since the seam in the cave had obviously been worked, at the very least by the long dead Lost Spaniard of the legend, there must have been some gold safe to take out.

Since Bandy had been prepared to part with the mining rights for what was comparatively little money, Carnigan reckoned he had already worked the seam until he did not dare do so any longer, and then tried to sell it to Hoffman.

He had counted without Hoffman's

hunger for money. Hoffman wanted the mine, all right, but he had no intention of paying for it. Carnigan had not known the saloon owner for long, but he had learned that much, at least: Hoffman never paid for anything.

But if Carnigan knew that, so did Pritt. He was no innocent ally in Hoffman's schemes. He must be a willing henchman at the very least, and, at the worst, a partner. The setup would have been perfect. Barkeeps were notorious for their big ears and interested attention to the doings of their customers.

Carnigan glanced at Pritt and found the man watching him carefully. Something was going unsaid in this. Something important and which affected the situation here.

He looked Pritt over carefully. For a man who had been caught in a major tunnel collapse, Pritt seemed remarkably little damaged. Scraped and scratched, yes. Covered in grazes under the coat of dust and muck, but not

175

seriously damaged in any way. No broken bones that could be seen, no serious wounds.

Not badly injured. Strong enough, for instance, to support his own weight by hanging onto the edge of the crater when the boulder had been dislodged. Not many perfectly healthy men could do that for very long without their grip failing. Carnigan worked with strong, rebellious horses all his life, and his grip and upper body strength were formidable. How come Pritt had the same kind of strength when the heaviest thing he lifted in his normal day was a bottle?

He pulled himself to his feet and leaned over to inspect Pritt, who looked back at him warily.

'Reckon you're strong enough to walk awhile?' Carnigan said. 'Time we was goin'. There was Apaches here this mornin' and I ain't got no idea where they went.'

Pritt agreed with surprising speed. He came to his feet sprightly enough, and stamped his feet to settle his boots back into place. No sign of weakness there.

'Long as we can take it in turns with the horse,' he said. 'I reckon I can keep up all right. Let's go!'

Taking it in turns with the horse was not in Carnigan's mind, but he decided it was better not to let Pritt know about that until it was absolutely necessary. He mounted, pointed ahead, and said, 'Lead off!'

He would have dearly liked to find out what was at the bottom of the hole Pritt had just used to return to life, but the idea of leaving Pritt on the surface with his horse while he climbed down into the depths was not a starter.

'I'll foller you,' Pritt told him, and Carnigan's suspicion was confirmed.

'No, mister, you lead on,' he said. 'You was too ready to see off that old miner for my liking. I want you where I can see you.'

'What if them Indians come back?'

'Me, I'm goin' to ride for it. You better get practisin' your Apache, mister!'

11

It took long hours to chivvy the complaining Pritt along the trail towards Sidewinder Flats and, by the time he had pushed the barkeep that far, Carnigan was on the brink of shooting the man himself, simply to shut him up.

When they finally found Hoffman's buckboard standing in a little draw off to one side of the trail, Carnigan heaved a sigh of relief.

'Your boss can't be far,' he told the bartender. 'Get in. He'll give you a ride back to town.'

Pritt glared at him sullenly. 'How do I know that?' he asked. 'Could be he's dead. Could be — '

'Could be I'll plant you myself, if you don't shut up,' Carnigan told him. He raised the reins and clucked the horse into motion, but took it up the draw instead of along the trail. When he topped out, he looked back to see that two men — Hoffman and Pritt — were now standing by the buckboard. Both were looking after him, and he waved his hat at them as merrily as he could manage, and rode on along the long ridge to town.

He still thought he had been mad to rescue the treacherous bartender, but he was unwilling to leave any man to die simply because of his own inaction.

On the other hand, he had been robbed of his hard-earned horses, ambushed and bushwhacked, hunted around town, been nearly buried alive in a collapsing gold mine, and a dishonest saloon keeper had tried to ambush him.

In a cold, calculating, controlled way which was far more dangerous than red-hot rage, Carnigan was beginning to get mad.

He rode his horse into the livery stable, unsaddled him and left him in a stall with a bait of feed, and a bucket of water. The old ostler who ran the stable looked him over and without speaking brought him a cup of coffee strong enough to float a paddle steamer. Carnigan took it gratefully.

'Hoffman back in town?' he asked. The old soldier shook his head.

'If he'd come in, I'd ha' seen him,' he said. 'Leaves his rig in his own stable, but he can't get there without bein' seen.'

He jerked his head towards the hay loft. 'You looked whacked,' he said. 'Was I you, I'd take an hour or so o' sack time. You can bed down in the loft. I'll tip you if Hoffman or one o' his gunnies comes a-lookin'.'

Carnigan believed him, and threw his blanket roll into the hay, and followed it up. It was late afternoon by the time he surfaced again, with the smell of strong coffee in his nostrils, and the old ostler grinning down at him.

'They're back,' he reported. 'Come in an hour ago, lookin' pretty goddam sick and sorry for theirselves, too. Hoffman and that barman of his went straight to the Hoffman House. Buchan and Gutierrez have finally come to open war. Gutierrez is down the end of town at the Mex cantina with what's left of his bunch after the Apaches had finished with 'em.'

'Apaches? I thought they drove them off.'

'Hit 'em on the way back into town, and left 'em pretty bad off.'

'Buchan?'

'He's at the Hoffman House. Got a new recruit, but he needs him too. Name of Juan. He fell out with Gutierrez.'

'So what are they doin' now?' Carnigan sipped from the coffee.

'Search me. No movement to speak of, though they got sentries out at the saloon. Town's quiet. The miners up from Ajo are back from the day shift; night shift went off ten minutes back in the wagons. What you figure to do?'

Carnigan swallowed the rest of his coffee and reached for his boots.

'Do? Well, first off I'm goin' to stand

myself some new duds to replace this lot I like to ruined. I'm goin' to get me a steak a foot thick and some fries to go with it and a few eggs on top. Then I'm goin' to tear down that bastard's smoke house, and clean up this town.'

The old man tittered like a girl, exposing a ragged array of teeth, and picked up Carnigan's coffee cup.

'Ain't had this much fun in a whole heap o' years!' he chortled. 'You fly right at it, boy! I'll watch your mounts here.'

*　*　*

Abraham was still in his store when Carnigan walked in through the make-shift morgue and clattered his Winchester on the counter. The man's eyes widened when he saw Carnigan's torn and dirty outfit.

'What the hell happened to you?' he asked, and Carnigan waved down his questions.

'Tell you later, Leo,' he said. 'Right

now, I need a bath, a set of new clothes from the skin out, and a couple boxes of .44s.'

The water was cold, but it refreshed him and wakened his senses. The new clothes felt good, and he had deliberately picked a dark colour shirt and jeans so he would not show up in the dark.

He pulled on his old vest and settled it into place while he walked down to the eating-house. There were some miners and a couple of ranchers and their wives eating in there, and Jenny served his coffee and food while hissing warnings at him.

He gathered he was insane to come back here, that both the Gutierrez and the Buchan factions were lying in wait for him and Hoffman was offering a dead or alive price on his head.

He shovelled down steak and eggs while she talked, and was washing it all down with another mug of coffee, when one of the miners got up to leave and paused at the door.

'There's men waitin' down the street with rifles!' he warned, looking at Carnigan.

It was only to be expected. In the darkness the word must have got round and somebody — likely Hoffman, who had most to hide — was out after him again.

He stood up and rapped on the table with his handgun.

'Sorry to interrupt your food, folks,' he said loudly. 'But seems like there's goin' to be some shootin' here soon. Seems to me it's goin' to be safer goin' out the back. If you'll just keep your heads low, and crawl out through the kitchen!'

He herded them out through the rear door, and was relieved that they were not met with shooting. Jenny protested at being sent off with them, but he snapped at her, and she went.

The trouble with the restaurant was that the men outside could see in and they were looking from the dark into a lighted room. He crawled from one lamp to another, extinguishing them.

Finally there was only the ghostly bluish light from the spirit lamp under the coffee urn on the counter. He crawled to the door and eased it open enough to see across the street.

There was a man on the sidewalk outside the Hoffman House, with a shotgun. By twisting his neck Carnigan could see along the front of the restaurant to one corner. He was turning away when he realized that he could see the reflection of the restaurant in the windows of the general store opposite. As he looked, a light flared at the side of the reflection, and he knew there was one man at each of the corners of the building. Two at the front, then.

And at the back? They might not have shot at the other customers, but they would certainly shoot at him. It was impossible that they had not posted a guard there.

In the gloom, the light of the spirit lamp seemed brighter and, as he glanced up at the ceiling, he saw there was a trapdoor there, almost over the counter.

The restaurant was unusual in that it had a peaked roof, rather than the flat one common in the town. So there would be a roof void up there.

He stood on the counter and reached up to push the trap open. It slid back easily enough, and he pushed his rifle through and laid it on the rafters. Then he stepped down from the counter, got a large frying pan from the kitchen and tiptoed to the back door, which stood ajar.

He threw the door open and threw the frying pan across the alley where it hit the fence and fell into a pile of cans, making a satisfactory din. He swore loudly, slipped back across the kitchen and stepped first onto the counter, then hauled himself through the trap and slid the cover back into place.

In the thick darkness, the outline of the trap showed up clearly as a ghostly blue line.

Outside, men shouted and two shots were fired. Then the back door slammed open and there was a crash as something was knocked over. A man swore luridly and then there was more shouting.

'Place is empty,' said one hoarse voice. 'Must have been him out back!'

There was an indistinct reply of which he could make out nothing, then the man in the kitchen said, 'Nothing here. I'm comin' out. Don't shoot!' and the back door slammed again.

He waited for a few seconds, then eased back the trap and stuck his head through. The room seemed to be empty, so he dropped his legs through, As he did so, a voice said triumphantly, 'Gotcha!'

His shoulders and one arm encumbered with the rifle were still stuck in the trap,and only his legs swung clear, but he could hear the unmistakable sound of a gun being cocked. Desperately, he swung his legs in an arc, connecting as he did so with the coffee urn. It fell backwards into the kitchen, and there was a curious muffled 'whoof!' and the light flared suddenly. He let go of the trap and fell through half across the counter, then to the floor of the main room.

A hair-raising thin screaming was coming from the kitchen and, as he sat up, he could see a man covered in blue flames slapping frenziedly at himself and staggering around the little room. He knocked over a can standing by the stove, and yellow flames joined the blue. The can must have contained oil, and it went up in a fountain of fire.

The burning man was shrieking on a high-pitched note. Carnigan shot him through the head, and threw himself out of the front door. He heard shouts and shots were fired, though none of them came near him.

He saw another man standing on the boardwalk in front of the Hoffman House, and snapped a shot at him which knocked the man off his feet and off his aim at the same time. Another came running from the alleyway down the side of the restaurant, and Carnigan shot again and missed. The running man simply continued across the street and disappeared down the side of the Hoffman House.

The flames inside the restaurant must have found some other source of fuel, for there was a loud explosion, and fire burst through the windows and the roof at the same time.

By now, the citizens of Sidewinder Flats were awake to their danger, and the street was filling rapidly with men in their longjohns and jeans, and women shepherding children away from the fire.

The wood from which most of Sidewinder Flats was constructed had been sitting out in the desert for a long time in a climate in which wood dries out within weeks. The whole town was tinder dry and the buildings were huddled together along the main street and even more crowded in the shanty town behind.

Within a surprisingly short time, the citizens had organized a bucket chain from the water tanks, and water was on its way to the flames.

Across the street from the restaurant, the imposing front of the Hoffman House stood out a garish red from the reflection of the fire, but otherwise, it seemed to be invulnerable to the drama being played out on the far side of the street. Carnigan could put that right.

12

The citizens of Sidewinder Flats knew just what a fire and a light wind would mean in their wooden town. There was no need to call them out: every man, every woman and even the few children of the town were out on the street.

Within a few minutes, a steady stream of buckets was passing along the chain and pouring onto the flames.

The more sensible people ignored it, and threw themselves on the building next to the flaming eating-house which was a boarding-house for the miners who used Sidewinder Flats as their base. Miners and cowboys wielding axes from the store and from their own supplies tore into the building which was already beginning to smoulder from the heat of the burning restaurant. A few of the more pessimistic ones ignored that in turn and fell upon the next building along which was so far protected from the flames. It was a feed store, and not as strongly built.

It was not long before the flames had gained a hold on the unlucky boarding-house and that, too, was up in flames. The fire fighters transferred their attention to the feed store instead.

Carnigan ignored them all, and crossed the street to the Hoffman House. Standing four-square opposite the fire, it was painted a deep, infernal red by the flames, so the internal lighting looked a garish yellow. A couple of the bar girls were standing in the doorway watching the fire fighters.

Carnigan remembered what Jenny had told him about Hoffman's recruiting techniques, and was not surprised that the girls did not move a finger to help. They simply stood and gazed at the efforts of the amateur fire fighters. They also ignored Carnigan as he walked across the street in the leaping fantastical shadows, and made his way past the Hoffman House and down a side alley. At the rear of the saloon was a corral, a stable and some sheds containing feed, Hoffman's buckboard and the stock for the saloon. The two gangs of toughs Hoffman kept at hand also stabled their horses there. Like most outlaws, they had excellent riding stock, and often needed it.

The light of the burning buildings did not seem to be getting any less, which told him the fire fighters were not being effective. The amount of shouting from the street had certainly got louder.

He eased round the corner of the saloon and peered down the rear wall, There was a rear door which led out to the corral and stables, and it was standing open. So far as he could see, through the glass panel in its upper half, there was nobody on guard on the far corner of the building, which surprised him.

Easing away from the saloon, he checked the stables. There were a few horses there, but not as many as he had expected. He left the stable and was about to walk across the corral to the rear door, when a man coughed, gently, in the dark. Carnigan was standing by the corner post of the corral and he hunkered down on his heels and looked carefully along the rails.

At the corner nearest the rear door, there was an indistinct shadow which thickened the outline of the corner post. As he watched, it moved slightly and the cough came again. The smoke from across the street was obviously catching in somebody's throat.

Where there was one man, there might easily be two or three, but time was scurrying past. After the big flare-up from across the street the light from the flames was already dying down. Not a sudden extinction, but a definite reduction in the intensity of the fire.

If he was going to move, he would have to do it fast.

He sidled up the side of the corral until he was crouching almost within arm's reach of the sentry. The man was restless, and shifted his position a couple of times, glancing round him in the gloom. How the man had missed Carnigan when he was crossing to the stable, Carnigan had no idea.

Carnigan could see from the outline against the light from the main street that he was wearing a sombrero. He was lying in wait, but was it for Carnigan or a member of the rival gang?

It did not really matter, Carnigan decided. He rose silently behind the man and reached for the sombrero, pistol ready to hammer the man over the head, when there was the sound of footsteps within the saloon, a glow of light as an internal door was opened and closed, and the sound of heels on the steps.

The Mexican stood up to his full height, and called out, 'Esteban?'

The newcomer grunted in return, and a match flared. Cigar smoke drifted invisibly across the open space, a strong contrast with the odour of burning wood from the flaming buildings.

'Did you get him?'

'No. He was in the street and we could see him. Then the smoke came down, and then he was gone. Keep a good watch here. He might try round the back.'

'If I see him, should I bring him in?'

'No,' said Esteban, casually. 'Kill him, then come in. This has gone on long enough.'

He turned back into the saloon and the door closed behind him. Carnigan was reaching out again, to remove the sombrero when the man saved him the trouble and removed the hat himself, and began fishing around inside it.

What he was looking for, Carnigan never found out. The action of tipping the hat to see inside outlined the outlaw's head against the glow of the dying flames, and he could never have asked for a clearer target. He smacked the Colt over the bent head as hard as he could, and the sentry dropped like a felled tree.

Carnigan waited for a second to see if anybody had been lurking in the darkness, but there was no outcry, so he dragged the man into the stables, used a lariat to tie his hands and feet to one of the stall dividers and gagged him with his own bandanna. Then he took the man's handgun and stuck it behind his belt at the back. The weight of three handguns dragging at his belt made him grateful for his habit of wearing his old cavalry suspenders as well as his belt, and the extra weight was, after all, only temporary.

He was gathering a heavy arsenal of artillery as he went on his way, but from the sound of things, he was going to need it.

The rear door of the saloon opened easily enough, and he stepped through it and flattened himself against the wall inside. There was another door, open, at the far side of the room, which appeared to be a store-room and had a floor cluttered with crates and barrels.

He crossed the floor and removed his

own hat before looking round the doorpost at knee height. He was looking, he found, into a small office with a high, roll-top desk, a cupboard which stood chest high, and two chairs. The room was too small to hold much else.

The noise from the street came more loudly here, and he crossed the room and peered through the far door into the saloon.

The place was almost empty and he supposed whatever men had been around had gone outside to help with the fire fighting. He could see the two girls standing in the doorway, still staring out at the street. One of them was smoking a cheroot.

A voice spoke from so close beside him that he flinched, then realized that the voice belonged to Hoffman, who was sitting at his usual chair under the balcony, and that the staircase was over Carnigan's head. The door in front of him was next to Hoffman's table in the void under the stairs, and Hoffman was sitting just outside it and to Carnigan's left.

'Did you check with Juan?' said Hoffman. There was a rumble of response from further away, and the saloon keeper growled testily. 'He's got to be somewhere around town,' he said. 'You did move his horse from the livery?'

This time the response was more testy. The strain of not knowing where he was seemed to be getting to them all, and he wondered for a moment why they should be so disturbed. Then he shrugged. Whatever the reason, it worked to his benefit.

He really needed to know how many men there were around the saloon and if possible where they were. Short of actually asking, he could think of no way of finding this out in the short time he had.

There was Esteban, who had come to check on Juan, the one currently talking to Hoffman, and if they had a sentry at the back they would be sure to have at least one at the front and at least two upstairs. That made six including Hoffman himself. There were probably more.

Well, he thought, if fire had solved his problem in the eating-house, there was no reason why it should not do the same here in the spider's lair. It was time this place was cleaned out for good.

There was a lamp on Hoffman's desk with a full reservoir, and he lit the wick and stood it on top of the cupboard where he would be able to see it from out in the main saloon with the door open. From outside, he could hear the sounds of men moving around, and at least one pair of boots scraped on the floor upstairs, almost over his head.

'Any sign?' Hoffman called. The man upstairs made negative grunts, and his colleague agreed with him.

'Where the hell is he?' muttered Hoffman again, almost in his ear through the board wall.

'Maybe he ran for it? Coulda had a

spare horse down at the corrals,' said Buchan's voice, speaking for the first time and almost as close as Hoffman. So two men at least must be sitting at Hoffman's table.

'I don't think so. That bastard's the sticking kind. I've seen them before in here. Get their teeth into anything, and they hang onto it until it drops, or they do. No, he's around someplace and I won't rest till I know where. How's Juan doing outside?'

Esteban replied from further away. He had only just checked on Juan. Everything out there was hunky dory. Juan was a good man.

The fire outside was definitely dying down now. Once it had been put out, the first thought of the fire fighters would be something liquid to get the smoke out of their throats. Time to go.

Carnigan stepped with infinite care out of the back of the saloon and ran along the side of the building to the front. He knew that the sentry there was standing at the far corner of the saloon, looking across the street at the remains of the eating-house. Not an ideal thing for him to do since the flames would have ruined his night vision.

He did not notice for a moment when Carnigan stepped onto the sidewalk, and when he did, it was too late. He yelped, tried to bring his rifle round to fire, and was knocked off his feet by the impact of the .44 slug from Carnigan's carbine.

Carnigan worked the lever, and shot the man again as he started to fall, then stepped into the street and looked up at the balcony which ran across the front of the building.

He could see one of the sentries immediately; he threw a shot at him, then heard a shot from almost directly over his head. The slug smashed into the street by his foot and he fired back at the muzzle flash, heard a grunt and a clatter as the man above dropped his rifle.

The other sentry had vanished.

Whether he had been hit and fallen out of sight, or merely startled enough to jump for cover, Carnigan had no way of telling. At any rate, he was not to be seen.

The two bar girls, who had been looking through the doors, though, were to be both seen and heard. One was screaming like a steam whistle, the other prudently threw herself off the sidewalk and ran for the darkened end of the street. The screaming girl, seeing her good example, ran after her, still screaming.

The batwing doors, still swinging from the girls' flight, were the obvious entrance to the saloon, so it made sense that the men within would expect him to come through it, so he stepped up on a box on the sidewalk, and kicked in the window. He had been intending to throw himself through it, but there was the roar of a shotgun from within the room, and the remains of the window suddenly erupted into the street.

One shot. There was another barrel

to come. He threw himself off the box and, in almost the same movement, through the doors.

The second barrel took out one of the batwings as he rolled as fast as he was able across the room and behind an overturned table. Bullets ripped splinters out of the woodwork as he did so and, when he was behind the solid, wooden tabletop, they came through that as well. He had heard somewhere that a .45 slug would go through four inches of pine and he promised himself he would never hide behind a table again.

The nearest alternative cover was the bar itself. He threw himself at the gap between bar and wall, and was behind the counter unscathed. For a moment, he wondered about the bullet-stopping properties of mahogany, when a slug came through one of the panels, spraying him with splinters, and he stopped wondering.

On his way across the floor he had seen there was one man on the landing over Hoffman's alcove and assumed it was the missing man from the upper storey; the man had been leaning over the balcony rail, shooting down at him. He glanced into the mirror over the centre of the bar and found himself looking straight up the barrel of a gun.

He ran, crouching, along behind the bar as bullets ripped through the woodwork. When he arrived at the serving door at the end, he stood up with a pistol in each hand, and shot first at the man on the balcony and Buchan, who was rising from behind Hoffman's table.

The first shot missed Buchan, though his second one caught Esteban, who was reloading the shotgun. Carnigan had not even heard the shotgun fire since he came into the saloon, and assumed he had missed the explosions in the barrage of shots which had missed him in his progress across the room. He shot Esteban just as the man snapped the gun closed again, and turned it towards the bar. The gun went off into the ceiling of the alcove, catching the upstairs sniper as he leaned on the balustrade to shoot at Carnigan, and the second slug from the Colt took out the Mexican's eye. As Esteban fell, the second barrel went off. Where the shot went, Carnigan had no idea, save that it did not hit him.

He found himself now faced with Hoffman and Buchan. Hoffman was moving extremely fast for a man of his bulk. Carnigan was not surprised, since he had seen the saloon keeper in action before, but he was surprised to see the man making for the door to his office, instead of joining in the gunplay.

He swung the borrowed .45 towards Buchan, to find the thickset man already halfway across the saloon floor toward him. The man was carrying a Bowie knife in his right hand, and the discarded shotgun in his left, held across his body like a bar.

Carnigan was desperate to get after Hoffman, but Buchan was too close to ignore, and moving too fast to be deflected. He cocked the .45 and pulled the trigger, only to hear the hammer fall with a click on an empty chamber. Then Buchan was upon him.

Carnigan threw the empty revolver at Buchan's head, and saw it draw blood on his cheekbone, but Buchan just shook his head and kept coming. The .44 was empty, and before Carnigan had time to reach behind himself and pull the third weapon, Buchan came over a table at him like charging bear.

He was moving fast, and swinging the empty shotgun with one hand and the Bowie with the other. But it was his cleated boots that took Carnigan's attention, and one of them was already swinging towards his head.

Buchan balanced instinctively on the centre of the table, and kicked like a dancer, leg straight and the massive boot travelling like a cannon ball. Carnigan twisted desperately, straight into the butt of the shotgun Buchan was wielding with his left hand. It caught him a glancing blow since he was already moving, but even so, the impact made his head resound, and slowed him down.

Buchan took advantage of the moment, slashing with the Bowie. Carnigan felt a line of fire run along his cheekbone. Hot blood spread down his cheek and into his collar, and the man on the table snarled like a wolf and swung with both hands at once.

It was a mistake. He could have used his feet again, but he had already felt the table top shift with the impetus of his kick, and he was not sure of his footing.

Carnigan saw the advantage and, instead of dodging back, he dropped his shoulder under the double swinging weapons, and hit the table with his hip. It tipped and the movement unbalanced Buchan. He dropped the shotgun and grabbed at Carnigan's head.

What his intention was Carnigan could not tell, but he knew this was his only opportunity to avoid those heavy boots, and he took it.

He ducked his head into his shoulders, took the thrust of the knife into the pad of muscle in his left shoulder, and leaned against it so that Buchan could not withdraw it. The pain flared as the point of the knife bit in, but it was into muscle, not bone.

Buchan, with his right hand and weapon immobilized and his feet travelling out from under him as the table tipped sideways, was already falling. Carnigan stepped back and let him tumble, away and on to the floor. The knife slipped out of the wound.

With his right hand he reached behind him and pulled the third pistol from the back of his belt. It was an old Civil War Remington and heavy as a club, but it delivered a .44 slug like the kick from a supply train mule.

Buchan saw it. His eyes widened a little and, for the first time, he reached for his own handgun which had been tucked away behind his belt buckle. But he was in the process of sitting up, and his own body was blocking the draw. As he dragged at the butt, the hammer spur caught in a fold of his shirt, and he fumbled for a second. It cost him his life.

Carnigan, shooting from the hip, put his first bullet into the man's chest, and his second through the gaping mouth. Buchan's head snapped back and a spray of red stained the upturned table top behind him. He was dead before his body slid sideways to the floor.

That still left Hoffman. Carnigan turned towards the door behind the man's card table. Hoffman had run for shelter in his office, and he had left the door open as he did so. Carnigan could not see the man, but he could see the lighted lamp standing on the cupboard in a line with the door.

He noted almost with detachment that the cupboard doors were open, and there was a darker space behind them. Then he pulled the trigger and the table lamp turned into a flower of flame which expanded frighteningly fast.

He turned on his heel, and looked

around the saloon. What had until half an hour ago been an opulent rich establishment was a shambles. Dead men seemed to be everywhere. Broken furniture was strewn across the floor, and the polished, heavy bar was riddles with holes.

The flames from the office were coming through the door now, and there was a succession of small, muffled explosions from the rear. From the half seen spurts of blue flame, he realized that there had been bottles and casks of spirit stored there, and they were, one at a time, exploding and spreading burning splashes around them.

He started to walk out of the door and stumbled as he went. The dull, burning sensation in his face and shoulder was turning to pain as the shock wore away. He needed to stop the bleeding, and fast.

As he lurched through the remains of the batwing doors, he found himself facing a street full of people. Half of them were in their night clothes, which in Sidewinder Flats meant longjohns and boots, just as they had come from their beds to fight the fire.

They were smoke stained and weary, and looked completely incapable of fighting another fire.

One or two, though, started forward with buckets, but he waved them back.

'Let it burn!' he said hoarsely. 'Let the goddamn place burn out! If you want a saloon, build a new one, and make it clean.'

Somebody shouted, 'It's the new sheriff!' and several started forward. Carnigan reached for his remaining gun, but then realized that the strange wave of sound he could hear was cheering. They were cheering him — the man who had burned down half their town.

With the sound in his ears, in a street lit by the flames of fires he had started, he slid gently into unconsciousness.

13

In his dream, tiny leprechauns attacked his shoulder with spears sharp as needles, and he came back to consciousness to find the needles were real even if the leprechauns were not.

'Keep still!' Jenny Rennes said testily, as he tried to roll on his back and sit up. 'I've nearly got you finished.' The pricking went on and he kept still with an effort while she completed the treatment. Finally, she slapped him on the back and said, 'You're done. Up you get since you're awake.'

Painfully, he rolled onto his back and swung his legs off the bed. His cheek felt stiff. When he touched it, he found that it had been stitched neatly and the wound was closed. He swung his head and looked at the woman questioningly.

'I stitched you up,' she said. 'May not be a surgeon, but you've met plenty of those in your time and, from the looks of it, some of them would do better in an abattoir. You've been wounded a lot.'

'Goes with the territory,' he admitted. His voice croaked because his mouth felt drier than the desert outside. Wordlessly, she pushed a pitcher of water at him, and he drank deeply. It helped.

'How long have I been in here?' he asked. As he spoke, it occurred to him that he had no idea where he was, and a cursory look around in the lamplight did not much help. He was in a square room, with wooden walls, a bookcase down one side, and a single chair standing by a stove in the corner. The bed was a double one, with brass head and foot. The sheet was stained with blood: his own.

'You're in my bed, in my shack,' she said. 'I refused to sleep in Polly's because it was too easy to get into. Didn't want every drunk in town rolling out of the Hoffman House and beating on my door. Here, I have my back to the rocks and a shotgun by the bedhead.'

He glanced over his shoulder, and saw she was telling the truth.

'The furniture is mine. It was a way of saving it from the thieves. Does that cover everything?'

Most of it, though he still did not know how long he had been unconscious. Not long, he thought, since he had not yet stiffened up, and experience said he would.

'Let me look?' She stooped over him and examined the face wound. It felt like a line of fire, but he had to admit that fire was not as hot and angry as he had expected.

'What did you put on it?'

She grinned. 'Indian balm. We get a few Pimas through here from time to time, until some yahoo drives them out. I did one a favour and he gave me a pot of it. I don't know where the pot came from, but it looked old.' She handed him a little brown clay pot with a twirling pattern cut in the surface.

'It comes from before the Navajo and the Apaches, I reckon,' he said, wondering. 'If I'm right that pot could be a lot of years old, ma'am. I guided a party of scholars one season, up towards the canyon. They was lookin' for this kind o' thing, and lookin' real hard. When they found a few fragments, they'd like to throw a party!'

She looked at the pot in wonder. 'Many years? Surely not!'

He grinned. 'That's what I thought, but then I never had no schoolin' except what my ma taught me, back home in Ireland. She said every man should be able to read and write and do figurin', and she sure made us study on 'em.'

'Must have been hard?'

'Ma's hand was harder. She said: 'you learn' — you learned. Glad she did now, but I didn't like it much at the time.'

'What are you going to do now? The Hoffman House is just a heap of ash. Half the men who were still here filtered out during the night. I heard them starting to leave even before the fires started. Was that you, by the way?'

'Guess so, ma'am. Seemed to me this town would benefit from a mite of replannin', so I did it.'

She stared at him. 'Half the town!' she exclaimed. 'You burned down half the town!'

He nodded modestly, 'That I did, ma'am. If I got half of it down, I reckon I done my job. They asked me to clean the place up, and fire they tell me has a cleansing hand.'

'So what happens now?'

He worked his arm experimentally. The wound in the shoulder burned like fire, but his muscles were responding well enough to control a horse, at any rate. Any cow pony was used to being controlled by the rider's knees to leave a cowboy's hands free for his roping. He could do what was necessary with his right.

'This wound go deep, ma'am?'

She shook her head. 'The one in your

shoulder is only shallow. Runs along the outside of the muscle under the skin. It bled a lot, that's all. Your face wound you can see for yourself. Long but shallow, as well. He can't have got a good swing at you.'

It felt as though he had been slashed by a dragoon with a blunt sabre, but certainly no muscles had been damaged, or he would not have been able to use the arm at all. His face wound felt inflamed and stiff, but, from its feel, she was right and it was superficial.

But he still had to find Hoffman and to round up the horses and drive them back.

'I got some horses to find and deliver to the US Cavalry,' he told Jenny. 'Know of anybody in this town who would make an honest wrangler? There's a lot of those ponies, and they're liable to be ornery.'

She was already packing clothes into a set of saddle-bags. 'You want a good wrangler, you're looking at her!' she told him. 'I grew up running around horses.'

It surprised him, but then most of the things this remarkable woman did surprised him — to the point where he should really not be surprised at all. He nodded and shrugged on his blood-stained shirt.

The dawn was just greying the sky when they let themselves out of the shack. She took a last look around at the few things she had salvaged from her marriage; there was a moment when her lower lip quivered, but she shrugged and turned away with a set face.

He was fully expecting all the horses to be gone from the stables, but there were still a few in the stalls and a handful in the corral out back, standing with their heads cocked and ears pricked. The fire must have put them on edge, he supposed, but there had been no sign of panic.

The old man was good with his horses. He was up already, forking feed into the mangers and spreading it on the ground for the stock in the corral. He glanced up as Carnigan and the woman walked through the stable and out the other end.

'Figured you for a dead 'un after that shootin' last night!' he said to Carnigan with surprise in his voice. 'How come you survived when so many died?'

'You complainin'?' Carnigan asked him testily. The shoulder was throbbing and his face felt as though he had been branded. He remembered the last time he had been scarred with a blade and knew he had days of this to come.

'Hell, no!' The old man walked into one of the stalls and came out leading Carnigan's horse, still saddled and with its saddle-bags intact.

He ran his eye over Jenny Rennes in her skirts and with the saddle-bags over her shoulder.

'You'll need a saddle, Jenny,' he said. 'Goin' far?'

'Far as I can and then some,' she told him tartly.

He gave a wheezy laugh. 'Be surprised how many citizens taken the same attitude,' he said. 'The Abraham couple decided to stay, and they been makin' themselves a fortune in the night, sellin' their saddles and campin' gear.'

'What do you reckon will happen to the town, now?' asked Carnigan. 'Without Hoffman to pull it together?'

'Mister, this town just set off into the desert only a few hours ago,' said the old man. 'Some'll make it; some won't, by the way they're treatin' their stock. Nobody won't come back, here. Only Hoffman kept 'em here in the first place, and without him, why stay?'

'And you?'

'Mister, I was here afore that man come and I'll be here after he's dead. This here desert ain't that bad, when the worst thing you got to fear apart from Apaches is a few critters.

'No, sir! Once the humans has gone and us old desert rats can go back to sleepin' on a hot stone, life'll get a mite more tolerable!'

He was working while he talked. A saddle was tossed onto a horse, and the animal bridled up. He led it out for Jenny.

'Good horse, this, lass. Owner ain't got no more use for him, and you fed me often enough when I was short. I reckon you earned him. One more thing!'

He turned towards Carnigan and fixed him with a surprisingly steely eye.

'From here on in, you're in charge of this woman, mister. From what I hear, you got a decent enough reputation, and you sure as hell know your horses. You look after her and you'll both be all right.'

Carnigan was surprised. 'How do you know what kind of a reputation I got?' The old man gave one of his wheezing laughs.

'Rode with Crook at the end o' the War Between the States and I seen you then.'

He gave a wink which would have

made an elephant dizzy, and waved them out.

'Your horses are in the far corral, where the water comes in.'

'You wouldn't know where Hoffman is, as well?' Carnigan was half joking and he was surprised when the old man grinned up at him.

'He lit out for Yuma while the fire was still goin'. Don't believe it my own self, though.'

Jenny stared at him, disturbed. 'Why not?'

'Ain't in his character. That Hoffman's a good hater. Keep your eyes on the high ground!'

He stood and watched them ride off in the desert dawn, with the pink light of the first sunrise reflecting on their backs, and shook his head sadly,

'I recall when I was that age, old hoss,' he told the mount in the nearest stall. 'Weren't no gals like that one around for me. That there is a lucky young feller if he stays alive to claim it!'

14

The old man had been right about Hoffman, but he had been wrong about the place the man turned up. He was not waiting on the road to Gila Bend, but on the hillside just overlooking the corral where Carnigan's horses were penned up waiting for their drive to join the army.

Carnigan and Jenny rode up and looked the horses over, and Jenny whistled in wonder.

'There's over fifty of them here!' she exclaimed, wiping her brow with the back of her hand. 'Must have taken you a long time to collect them.'

Carnigan was counting them over carefully, tapping on his saddle for every count of ten. When he had got to five taps, he whistled.

'Every one of them here!' he exclaimed. 'Not a one missing. That's a miracle.'

Jenny was fiddling at her waist, then dismounted and dropped her skirt to the ground and stepped out of it. Under it, she was wearing a man's jeans. Even in his surprise over the herd tally, Carnigan found time to notice she filled those jeans very snugly.

'Easier to work horses without a skirt dragging around my feet,' Jennie explained, though she coloured very prettily. She twisted the skirt into a thick rope and slid it through the straps which held her bedroll, then remounted.

As she did so, she gave a sharp gasp, and Carnigan looked up find himself staring into the barrels of a shotgun.

Behind the shotgun was Hoffman and behind Hoffman was Hoffman's barkeep, Jed Pritt.

Carnigan cocked an eyebrow at Pritt.

'Well, well, it's Pritt the sleepin' partner,' he said. He hooked his knee over the pommel of the saddle, fished in his pocket to produce his tobacco sack, and started to roll himself a cigarette.

225

'I wondered where you was last night when the shootin' started. Packin' for the trail, Jed? Heavy, was it?'

He noticed Hoffman's eyes flicker when he said it, and wondered if all was well between the two men who had together run Sidewinder Flats. After all, just where had Pritt been when the lead started to fly? He certainly had not been in the saloon, and he did not look like a keen amateur fire fighter, so where had he been just at the time his boss needed him?

Jenny was like a statue, apparently caught in the act of mounting. She had one hand on the reins at the saddle horn, one foot in the stirrup and the other foot hanging loose down the side of the horse. To balance herself, she had put her free hand down on the back of the saddle, and it was still there, very close to the bedroll tied over the saddle skirt.

Pritt ignored her, and gestured at Carnigan.

'Get down!' he snapped. 'And keep

226

your hands away from your gun!'

Carnigan shrugged, his fingers busy building his cigarette. 'Give me a minute,' he pleaded. 'I've been gaspin' for a smoke all mornin'.'

Hoffman scoffed: 'Let the man have his smoke,' he said. 'It will be his last. And then we can deal with our local hash slinger the way she needs to be dealt with!'

Pritt's eyes turned ugly and he shot Jenny a glance which was like a threat. It was also a mistake. While his attention was even partly distracted, Carnigan finished his cigarette, twirled the end of it, and stuck it in his mouth.

He started to feel in his pockets for a match, and his hands worked down from shirt pockets to vest pockets, to his belt. Pritt started to say something, and Carnigan pulled his spare gun from behind his belt buckle and shot him in the chest.

The impact of the heavy, .44 slug fired at short range knocked Pritt half round, and his shotgun discharged into the ground, flinging a little cloud of sand and dust into the air. Carnigan shot him again, and started to pull his gun round to deal with Hoffman, sickeningly aware that he had to be too late. The saloon keeper was already pointing the shotgun at him.

Carnigan heard the sound of the shot, curiously muted, as he dropped off the far side of the horse, and rolled over to fire his Colt between the animal's feet towards Hoffman.

But the man was already falling away from him, and he heard once again the curiously muted explosion, and this time correctly placed it as coming from Jenny.

She was standing in her stirrups, with one arm extended towards Hoffman, and there was a cloud of powdersmoke around her hand.

The whole event happened so quickly that Carnigan was already climbing back to his feet as Hoffman hit the ground on his back.

The stock in the corral, spooked by

the unexpected shots, began to run around the enclosure.

Jenny dismounted and hung onto her mount's reins while it calmed down. Carnigan tied his horse to the top rail and bent over Pritt. The man was not dead, but he was obviously dying, and the venom was still in his eyes.

'Luck!' he croaked. Blood was soaking the front of his shirt, and bubbling in his mouth. 'Pure luck! I had you dead to rights and you damn well know it!'

Carnigan nodded, his eyes like flint.

'I was lucky enough to be faster than you, even when you got the drop, Jed,' he said. 'You need . . . '

But he was talking to a corpse. The hating eyes slid off to one side, and the blood trickled out of the dead mouth and down the cheek.

Jenny was bending over Hoffman, but as Carnigan walked over to her, she looked up and shook her head. The saloon keeper was obviously dying, and there was blood in the sand under his neck.

He stared at Carnigan when the man leaned over him and it was clear he was struggling to ask a question.

'Who . . . who *are* you?' he said. 'Who sent you after me? Bell? De Soto? Who?'

'Nobody had to send me. I'm just a man come for his horses, you thievin' bastard,' Carnigan told him. 'If you'd left me alone, you'd still have your thieves' paradise here. You stick your hand in a rattler's hole, you get bit!'

Hoffman shook his head. 'Can't be just happenstance! There's something . . . ' Then he, too, was gone.

Carnigan straightened up, and stared down at the two corpses, then turned his gaze to Jenny. She was still holding a pistol in her hand, a heavy, bulky revolver which looked far too big for her. She looked up and caught his eyes upon hers, and shrugged.

'It was my husband's. The one he wasn't wearing when he needed it,' she told him. 'I practised with it over the past year so I could use it instead. And I did.'

'You certainly did,' he told her. 'You saved both our lives with that — and I owe you in spades, for it.'

'Think nothing of it,' she said shortly. 'Now, let's get these horses of yours on their way.'

So they did.

THE END

We do hope that you have enjoyed reading this large print book.

Did you know that all of our titles are available for purchase?

We publish a wide range of high quality large print books including:
Romances, Mysteries, Classics
General Fiction
Non Fiction and Westerns

Special interest titles available in large print are:
The Little Oxford Dictionary
Music Book, Song Book
Hymn Book, Service Book

Also available from us courtesy of Oxford University Press:
Young Readers' Dictionary
(large print edition)
Young Readers' Thesaurus
(large print edition)

For further information or a free brochure, please contact us at:
Ulverscroft Large Print Books Ltd.,
The Green, Bradgate Road, Anstey,
Leicester, LE7 7FU, England.
Tel: (00 44) **0116 236 4325**
Fax: (00 44) **0116 234 0205**